CHILDREN SHOULD BE SEEN AND NOT HEARD

Trisha McAfee

INTRO

Panic-stricken, I knew what was about to come next. I yelled at my attacker, to get off me, I was pregnant, but that did not matter to him. I felt the pull of my hair, his smelly breath, as he was yelling at me, and smashing my head against the floor. Just when I thought I was about to pass out. I heard a voice saying, "Don't give up! Get up!" When I saw my opportunity, I hit him as hard as possible.

He got off me gasping for air. There was only one way out, down the hallway to the back door. The only problem was there were no steps, I'd have to jump. I was five months pregnant visibly showing. I knew I had to jump, or I was going to die. I heard the pounding of his footsteps and him yelling, "Hey, kid, where do you think you're going you little bitch"! It was then that I jumped. I felt a pain in my stomach, but I ran to my car and left. Not long after, I finally braved enough courage to look up in the rearview mirror to see if he was behind me. The coast was clear, there were no signs of my father.

> *When asked how I lived in the company of monsters,*
>
> *I said, "they did not know they too were amongst a beast."*
>
> ***Author Lisa M. Lilith Ilmusings***

<u>*Words to Other Survivors*</u>

It's May 25, 2024, and as I write this story, I can't help but think that perhaps no one will ever read it, making this effort feel pointless. But if just one person does read this, and if you've walked a path like my characters, I hope my story of survival, pain, and eventual triumph reminds you that your journey isn't over yet. There is still hope.

If you are caught in the struggle of an abusive relationship, know that there is help available. No matter where you are, there are organizations dedicated to helping you and your loved ones find safety. It's never too late to seek help, and support is only a phone call away.

<u>The National Lifeline can be texted or called at 988 or chat at 988lifeline.org.</u>

<u>The National Mental Health Hotline is 866-903-3787.</u>

In Memory of

Tracy McAfee-White

June 12, 1972 — August 21, 2011

Chapter One

Early 80's

IT WAS A SPRING MORNING, on an isolated country road in the early eighties when the chaos roared through the run-down trailer. The trailer was a late 1950s double bedroom, single bath. The white exterior had rust stains over the siding and peeling paint, the windows had cracks in the glass, and the screens all had gaping holes. The steps leading to the porch were rotten throughout so badly you had to watch your footing, the porch had an old cast iron table and chairs, with some trash lying around, and the front door hung barely by the corroded hinges.

That spring morning started with screaming that echoed throughout the run-down home. There my father stood with the charcoal fluid in his hand as he poured it into the open stove. His six-foot-three stature towered over the stove. His long, mangy brown hair laid over the side of his face, his long beard was that of some rocker from a band, his ragged pajamas fit like highwaters on his lengthy legs, and his ripped dirty white t-shirt barely covered his pop belly. There my father stood, the first man who was supposed to protect us from any harm done, trying to throw matches into the stove where the freshly poured charcoal fluid lay. He tried lighting the stove, but the match blew out before touching the fluid.

The screams from our mother were high-pitched, almost piercing, yelling at us girls to run and get out of the disarrayed house. My sister grabbed me, almost throwing me to her hip. I had to of been around 3 years at the time. My night-grown bunched up around my upper thighs, I laid my head on her upper shoulder. I squeezed my eyes closely shut, as I could hear the yelling all around me. I held onto Kay with all my might. My body was trembling and so was Kay's. Lynn, the middle daughter, stood beside Kay, almost clinging to her. We were all

4

visibly shaking. Not sure of what to do, or too scared to move, Kay stood in the middle of the living amongst the toys scattered on the floor.

Just as we were about to leave, Father threw our mother at the door. He grabbed her by her white shirt, lifting her off the ground. His head touched her forehead as he held her against the door. I could hear the crackle of her voice as she said, "Randy, stop, put me down, you're hurting me"! The look of terror was written all over her face. Tears streamed down her already bruised and battered face. Her body was shaking uncontrollably over her hourglass frame. He stared back at her with emptiness in his eyes. It was the kind of emptiness that would bring chills down your spine. Her blue eyes swelled up with tears and they began to fall uncontrollably. "Randy, stop, you're scaring the girls!" Our mother said, gasping in between tears.

My oldest sister, Kay was carrying me and tried to push her way through, but he wasn't having it. He shoved her backward, causing her to fall onto the couch. She held onto me tight making sure not to lose her grip. My other sister Lynn stood there not knowing what to do. Father stood over her snarling, spitting coming from his mouth like a rabbited dog, all while he was screaming, "You little bitch I will fucking kill you! Do you fucking understand me? I will kill each of you little bitches! Father screamed angrily." Kay covered my face, her hands shaking, as she held me tightly.

My mother finally mustarded up the courage to shove him back, causing him to lose his footing, and fell to the dirty kitchen floor, merely missing the kitchen chair. He was taken aback by the look on his face, stunned, if I must say. However, his stunned look turned to anger, explosive at that. He let out an angry scream! "I'm going to fucking kill you all, my father snarled, hastily." He jumped to his feet and grabbed the matches that had been lying on the kitchen counter amongst the dishes in the sink.

It was then, that he did the inevitable, he grabbed the matches, throwing a lit match into the stove, but by God's miracle, it did not catch. "RUN", my mother screamed, "Run, for the car, don't look back, go, go, GO!!" She pushed the rusty screen door open, my sister carrying me behind, then Lynn behind her. Trying not to fall through the holes on the porch and the steps, Kay tried her best not to fall. However, her right foot slipped and pushed through the rotten wood on the step. Luckily, she was able to react fast and pull her leg out.

Normally the sandstone pathway didn't seem that long, but this day it was never-ending. The morning dew lay on the weeds and grass that was around the sandstones, causing it to be slippery. Finally, we made it to our Cutlas, the red seats were cold, and you could see our breath as my mother fumbled at her keys to start the car.

We heard the screams of our father coming closer. I tried popping my head up to see what the noise was. I was so young; it didn't dawn on me that the noise I was hearing was a shotgun. Kay grabbed my head and shoved it back down, tucking it away and against her chest. I could hear her heart beating; I would even say I heard it skip a beat. He was running towards the hillside on his bare feet, carrying his 22-riffle. Then, suddenly, we heard "BOOM, BOOM, BOOM!" Father stood on the hillside, with his 22-riffle, shooting at the car with everyone inside.

Sobbing could be heard throughout the car. It was a gut-wrenching sound. A sound that filled that musty-smelling car. It was a sound of defeat, shame, and courage or so I thought. Later, in life, I would learn my mother wasn't who she said she was at all. Finally, mother found the right key and started the car. Our mother sped down the dirt driveway, making a right down that back country road. Dirt and gravel flew up hitting the car, which caused a cloud of dust behind us.

God must have had bigger plans that day because no bullets hit the car where my sisters and I sat with our heads tucked down in hopes that we didn't get shot. Just shy of a mile, we heard a loud bang as the tire exploded from a stray bullet that grazed it, causing it to go flat. Mother jumped out of the car nervously looking down at the back driver's side tire back tire. It was going flat. She jumped back into the car, driving it on its rim for a couple of miles until we hit our Aunt Sara and Uncle Lawson's house.

Aunt Sara and Uncle Lawson's house was beautiful, it was an ordinary brick house. Unlike our own home, it was clean, it had a rose smell to it from the tart warmer sitting on the kitchen counter. He was a broker, and she was a stay-at-home mom. They had a unique L-shaped pool with an attached slide. A pergola off to the side with an attached pool house connecting to their garage. They kept their pool floaties, a bathroom was just ahead with a shower.

Later, that night against the wishes of my aunt and uncle we returned home, to the father, who tried killing us just that morning. After we walked into the dilapidated trailer one by one, we walked in like prisoners of our own home, not knowing what to expect. The lights we all off and as my mother turned the light switch on, their father sat in his favorite ratty-looking flowered chair holding his dog, Lady. She was a dachshund, red. Father had her before mother and he was married in 1977. He yelled at us to put our asses down on the couch, then began to tell Mother that if she'd ever pull a stunt like she did that morning again, or even speak of what happened that he would kill each of us and she'd be last so she could watch him put a bullet between each of our foreheads. We all sat motionless, too scared to move, too scared to even breathe too hard. We didn't speak of that morning again, until years later for fear he would live up to his promise of killing us all.

Chapter Two

So It Begins

MY NIGHT STARTED AS ORDINARY or as ordinary as a 5-year-old night could be. My mother and I had planned to watch The Wizard of Oz. Before the movie started, she bathed me in our lime-green bathtub. It had soap scum visible around the tub, even the ledges where we put our shampoo were filthy will soap scum. I sat there in the discolored water that hit just at my waist playing with my dolls. Mother came in, bent down, grabbed the cup that was on the edge of the tub, filled it with water, and began to wash my long blonde hair. The shampoo she was using filled the air, smelling like strawberries.

Afterward, I hopped into my nightgown and ran through the hallway with excitement jumping onto the flowered couch. I could smell the fresh popcorn that Mother had made on the stove. It made my mouth water. I yelled, "POPCORN, yummy! POPCORN, PORNCORN!" Mother brought in a bowl as I settled down. I sat there eating anxiously for the movie to start. Finally, the movie began, and we started to watch it. Everything seemed perfect. A great way to end the night. Or so it seemed. Evil would be lurking in the shadows, but my 5-year-old little body would learn how evil the world could be. Although I've already encountered more at 5 years old than most had by the time they die.

Shortly after the movie started headlights appeared in the driveway, it was Father coming home. He walked into the door; coal caked all over his face from hauling it that day for his customers. He was a jack of all trades as people would say. He hauled coal, picked up people's trash, cut firewood, and worked on vehicles. During the summer months, he would pick berries and apples, making some of the best cider around. My family relied on the money to pay our bills and to put food on the table. He didn't have a regular 9 am-5 pm like my friend's dads. He was uneducated and dropped out of junior high his eighth grade year, to help at his family's gas station. So, to make ends meet he did odd jobs.

"The Wizard of Oz," Father yelled. "I haven't watched this in a long time. Scooch over kid, I'll watch it with you" Father exclaimed. I scooched over excitedly that he wanted to watch the movie with me. He never wanted to watch a movie, let alone do anything with me. He wasn't like other dads who would play board games, throw the ball outside, and do dad's things. Most of the time he didn't have time or simply didn't want to make time. However, he was available for other family's children. Just never for us.

I lay frozen, laying under my favorite brown and white Afghan blanket, watching The Wizard of Oz. It was the scariest part of the movie when the witch was talking to Dorothy at the castle. I had my favorite Strawberry Shortcake nightgown and matching panties on. I thought it was going to be an ordinary night of watching TV. Little did I know how wrong I could be. I was only 5 years old; I had no clue what was happening to me, just knew it didn't feel right, it hurt. Laying there under the blanket with my father, he pulled me closer. I could feel his beard on the back of my neck and smelt his body odor from the day's work. His coughing could be heard echoing throughout the trailer. Although he wasn't a smoker, he had a cough like someone with COPD from the years working in the mine and hauling coal. His hand was on my hip holding me close, then it moved close to my thigh. I began to feel that something wasn't right, but I was only 5 years old. What's right and wrong? He was my father, he was there to protect me, right? I couldn't be more wrong. As I lay there, I then started to feel his hand slide behind my legs, then open my tiny legs up, enough that he could lay his hand in between my legs. His hand laid there for what seemed to be forever and perhaps if it did the next act wouldn't have taken place. He slid my Strawberry Shortcake panties to the side. I felt his fingers slide over my no-no zone, then again, and again. I started shaking, like someone who had been sitting outside when the weather was too cold, but I wasn't cold. I was scared, too scared to speak, too scared to voluntarily move, too scared to react to fear of his reaction if I did. My mind went blank, I didn't move, I could see, feel, and hear everything that was around me. I simply couldn't move. I was frozen solid in fear.

Then, when I thought it couldn't get any worse, I felt pain and pressure as his finger began to slide inside my body. I was so scared that I peed all over the couch, my favorite nightgown, and father." God dammit kid, what did you do that for, huh? What the fuck is wrong with you?" Father screamed. Mother jumped up, "What's wrong, what happened?" mother shouted. "This little bitch pissed all over me! What the fuck is wrong with her?" father shouted. I stood there unable to move, trembling, big crocodile tears rolling down my face, and still peeing on the floor. My parents looked at me with disgust and anger. "Get the fuck to the bathroom you little bitch, get the fuck out of here! Go, now!" mother snarled. I took off running to the bathroom and finished peeing in the lime green toilet. I couldn't breathe, from crying so much. I wasn't consolable when Mother finally came to the bathroom. The look of disgust and anger was obvious when she jerked me off the toilet, grabbed Father's belt that lay on top of the washer, and beat me with the belt buckle from the small of my buttocks to the bottom of my ankles. She repeatedly beat me until I couldn't take it anymore. I collapsed onto the floor. The vinyl floor was cold to the touch as my naked body lay there shivering, sobbing, and screaming in between tears.

The next morning when I woke up, I was still on the bathroom floor naked, cold, and dirty from laying on the floor the night prior. As I was lying on the floor just about to get up, I heard the door slam open. It startled me. I jumped up, holding onto my naked body. It was Father. "You little bitch what are you doing?" father screamed. He pulled at my arm and walked me to my bedroom my feet could barely touch the floor as he was dragging me down the hallway. I was all but running on my tip toes to keep up with him. He gets to my bedroom and throws me to the ground. There I lay in the mix of clothes and toys. "Get dressed you little bitch! Get dressed now!" father screamed. I jumped to my feet looking for the nearest clothes to throw on, a dirty rainbow sweatshirt, jeans that had holes at the knees, purple and pink socks, and a pair of white canvas shoes that were no longer white, but filthy from playing outside in the grass.

I'm not quite sure where Mother was that morning, there was no sign of her anywhere. "Hurry up kid, don't make me say it again!" Father said hastily, "I walked through the living room and glanced over at the couch that was now covered with the brown Afghan blanket from the night before walking past it ashamed and guilt-ridden. "How could I be such a baby to pee over my favorite nightgown, couch, and father?" I said quietly. Father stood there in the kitchen sink, opening a chocolate pop tart. I stood there eyeing up the chocolate that was smeared over the top. It was my favorite and father knew. "See, he's not mad at you!" I said to myself. My eyes grew bigger as he handed me the chocolate-glazed pop tart. "Here eat this, I shouldn't give you anything after the stunt you pulled last night!" Father said as his voice cracked. "Thank you, father. "I said in a whisper.

"Now, let's go you're going to cause me to be late!" Father said. We walked to the truck in silence, it was cold out that morning, and I could see my breath, I began to shiver as we walked closer to Father's blue pick-up truck.

13

"Get in we don't have much time, I already told you I'm going to be late! Dammit, kid, go, get inside! Sit your ass down and get your seatbelt on." Father snapped. "I fumbled trying to get my seatbelt buckled, but every time I went to move there was a horrible reminder of the night before. The pain was almost unbearable to sit through. Finally, after several attempts I got the seatbelt buckled.

I sat there finishing my pop tart looking out the window as Father backed his old Chevy out of the drive. It was so hard to sit still with the amount of pain I was in. I glanced down at my leg where my pants barely covered it. I leaned over and pulled back my pant leg to see a bruise that appeared. It was square like the belt buckle that mother used the night before. "Sit still kid or I'll give you something you can cry about!" Father said angrily.

Quietness filled the truck until we got to the coal mine. It was a bumpy ride; hills and hills of coal were all around us. Dump trucks were being filled up with coal at the coal house. Or at least that's what I would call it. Father pulled up to the farthest hill of coal, it looked like a mountain to my 5-year-old self. He shut the truck off got out and said, "Stay here, this won't take long. I'll be right back." Father started picking the best coal pieces he could find for his customers.

In the morning rush, I forgot my jacket from the closet, and with the truck being shut off I began to get cold. I sat there with my arms crossed as I looked out the window. Now and again, I'd take my hand and wipe off the window from the frost that was building up from being so cold out. I sat there and looked around the truck and found Father's old red flannel. I lay down and covered up, shivering. I fell asleep waiting for my father that morning, a mistake I wish didn't happen.

Father must've gotten back into the truck while I was still sleeping. I felt him grab my head and pull me closer placing my head on his lap. His pants were navy blue with coal-stained marks, he was wearing a green long-john top, and his steel-toe work boots that had holes throughout.

"Here, kid I have something for you, stay right there! Give me your hand and keep your eyes closed." Father said. I was so excited thinking he got me a candy bar; Hersey was the best. I keep my eyes closed tight, as he reaches, taking my hand. "Now, keep your eyes shut. Here take this and rub your hand on it like this. He made a back-and-forth motion with my hand. However, this wasn't the candy bar for which I was hoping. This was warm, round, and long like a hot dog. "That's right, like that!" Father said with almost a chuckle following. I thought to myself, how is this my surprise? What am I touching, this doesn't feel right. Then, a short time later, my father, let out a moan, saying, "Aww that's daddy's girl." I pulled my hand away because it was covered with something wet, warm, and sticky. I went to get up and he shoved my head back down. "Just lay there kid, go back to bed. You did daddy good" Father said.

Chapter Three

The Hanging

THAT BEAUTIFUL FALL AFTERNOON was a child's dream. The weather was amazing and perfect, not too hot, or cold. You could see some of the trees changing from bright vibrant green to hues of yellow, red, orange, and golden brown. It was just right. You could even smell the slightest hint of fall with the earthly scent of the newly decaying leaves.

Kay had been lying outside on the porch getting her tan. Her pasty white skin could use as much help as it could to achieve her gold brown as she wanted before that fall got too cold to lay. You could smell her tanning lotion from inside the living room. A common combination of baby oil and iodine was the perfect combination that Mother used to help turn her and Kay's body to the perfect golden brown. Kay's headphones were placed just right over her long blonde hair, and her sunglasses rested just on the bridge of her nose, as she listened to the latest eighty's hits on the Casey Kasem weekend radio show. A white boxed fan was placed just beside her cooling her body off as it blew her hair from time to time as it rotated. She laid on the brown Afghan blanket on her back with her arms out on each side and her left leg titled slightly upward. You could tell she was into the music playing as she bobbed her head back and forth with the occasional bubble being blown from her gum.

"Kay, can you watch the girls, I've got errands to run?" Mother said. "Sure, Mother where are you going?" Kay asked. "I've got to go downtown and pick up my Avon order, then bowling in Jewett after 5 pm. Tonight's our first practice for league." Mother said. Mother stood there over top of Kay as she was basking in the sun watching her blow bubbles in between their conversation. Mother stood almost annoyed at the sound of Kay's popping her bubbles. "Can you not do that while I'm talking to you? You sound like a cow!" mother exclaimed. "Yes, sorry mother." Kay's voice cracked as she whispered with almost embarrassment. "I'm going to get ready." Mother said. "Okay, sounds good. I'm going to pick my stuff up and head inside I've got school assignments to do." Kay said. Kay grabbed her belongings almost in discuss from the earlier conversation with her mother. As she was picking her tanning lotion up, she practically threw it into the Afghan, along with the fan, and her pillow. She balled up everything into the Afghan and then threw it over her shoulder like a ragdoll. She let out an "UGH" as the fan hit the back of her legs as she was reaching for the door.

Mother came out a short period later, her blonde hair curled, with her big fluffy bow being placed in the small of her neck, make-up added so perfectively highlighting her captivating blue eyes. Her eyes were an ice blue that could also pierce a person's soul. Her blue eye shadow blended precisely with her eyes; her mascara added so thickly you'd almost think the hair on his eyelashes were spider legs. It took away from her beautiful eyes, but she insisted on caking it on every time she wore it. Her red blush was boldly applied to her accentuating her already high cheekbones. Giving her the very iconic eighties look that all the women were wearing. Her black stirrup pants fit her hourglass body extremely tightly, causing her to have a muffin top or extra fat hanging over her pants. Her button-up shirt was white with mustard yellow, blue, and green stripes with her mustard yellow belt that accented her dress top just right. She of course matched her top to a T, mustard yellow, with a bow that sat right in the center with a silver buckle in the middle. She always had to have her shoes match her outfit, I guess it was part of her style. As she walked through the rundown trailer her vanilla perfume could be smelt throughout, to the point you could taste it I'd go as far as choking on it.

Kay was sitting at the kitchen table doing her math assignments. She just started her senior year and couldn't be more thrilled. Math, however, was a subject she always seemed to struggle with but managed to get passing grades. Kay glanced at Mother. "Wow, you look pretty," Kay said with a smile. "Thank you," mother said. "Umm where's the girls, Kay?" mother asked. "I'm not sure, outside playing maybe?" Kay said in an almost asking manner. Mother yelled for the girls, but nobody answered inside the trailer. She went inside the girl's bedroom, and they weren't there either. "I don't have time for this fucking shit, I have to get going or I'm going to be late!" Mother said angrily. Kay got up and stood on the porch, she yelled, "Girls, where are you?" But again, nobody answered. "This isn't funny, where are you? Girls, get up to the house right now! You're in big trouble!" Kay screamed. Finally, Kay heard muffles coming from the backyard. She walked over to the side of the porch and looked in the backyard. Kay screamed, "NO, no, no!!" What are you screaming about Kay?" Mother snapped. Then, she saw the inevitable herself. "NOOOOOOOOOOO!" mother screamed.

That day Lynn and I decided to play in the clubhouse. It was a dilapidated old chicken coop that Father turned the backside into the clubhouse. It wasn't anything fancy, our rabbits' cages were on top, their food containers off to the left side. There was a window straight ahead, without any glass, so you could feel the cold air. When it rains the rain often blows inside, causing the floor to get wet and slippery. The floor was made from scrap wood which had been lying around from other projects. You could often feel your weight give when you walked across the floor. In the summertime, the ceiling would often have flies and bugs of all sorts that would collect themselves throughout. It was nothing to see an occasional snake and certainly, you'd see an overwhelming abundance of rats. They would eat the rabbit's food, and although the food was in a container, they'd chew holes through often causing us to run out of food before mother and father could afford to buy more. During those times we'd often pick grass to feed them. I would watch with caution throughout the clubhouse for fear that I would have a snake just waiting for the perfect moment to wrap itself around me. Luckily, that never happened. However, there was a snake or two that would get inside and eat the chickens' eggs. The chickens were called Two and Foo. The turkey had the most original name of all, Tom. I would often go to the clubhouse by myself and talk to them like they were my best friends, the absolute best friends a girl could ever have.

Off the side of the clubhouse was a high side with a slight slope, there was a maple tree with an old tire swing and a longer rope attached that we would swing from. We used to pretend that we were Tarzan, screaming down, pounding on our chest till we almost hit bottom then let go. This day we were standing on the hillside and playing with the rope. I'm not too certain how but the rope ended up getting wrapped around my neck. It's been said that Lynn did it intentionally, but that's far from the truth. We were standing on the hillside and the next thing I knew I was hanging from the maple tree, my legs completely off the ground, I struggled to breathe, gasping for air, and grabbing at the rope to loosen it. I don't recall much but just went I went to lost conscientiousness Kay came running up through the yard and bear-hugged me lifting me. I could feel my weightlessness from my body, death knocking at my door, as Kay struggled to remove the rope from my neck. By the time Mother had gotten to us, she yelled at Kay to "Hold me up higher." Finally, Mother was able to help Kay remove the rope from my neck. I let out a weak gasp and sigh of relief, then burst into tears. My sister practically ran with me back down to the house Mother yelled angrily to Lynn, "Get your fucking ass down to the house, right fucking now! You little bitch! RIGHT FUCKING NOW! Lynn ran the fastest I ever saw that day. Her long black hair blew in the wind as she was running, and her knobby knees could barely keep up with her she fell onto her stomach and practically slid across the lawn. Lynn's feet flew up behind her almost causing her to flip over. You could tell that Lynn was out of breath, her frail body barely made it to the steps before she collapsed from exhaustion. There she lay on the bottom step winded, gasping for air in between tears and screaming that she was sorry. Her already pre-existent heart condition was worn on her allying body. She took medication daily to help keep her heart regulated. Lynn was 10 years old but looked to be a lot younger. Mother finally reached Lynn, not saying a word to her grabbed her by the hair, clinching her fingers as tight as she could make them. Mother started dragging Lynn's fragile body backward up the steps, hitting the small of her back on all three of the steps, and continued to drag her across the already fallen-in porch. It was then that Lynn's knee hit a nail that came loose. Lynn let out a scream of agony, and blood started gushing out, as she tried to tug at her knee and bring it closer. However, she couldn't do that, due to her mother dragging her faster than she could keep up. Mother finally reached the door; she practically threw it off the hinges with how hard she threw it open. Continuing to drag and throw Lynn around like a ragdoll, at last Mother stopped in the hallway. Lynn, lying there in a fetal position, dirty from head to toe from being on drugs, grass stains all over her blue shirt from falling, and some leaves that got tangled up in her hair. Without saying a word, mother stood over top Lynn drew her right foot back as if she was going to punt a football and kicked her in her chest causing her to slide into the wall. Mother repeated this act a few more times until Lynn was no longer fighting back. Blood was pouring from Lynn's mouth and nose.

Then, mother spit in Lynn's face. As she was walking away. She said, "Get up cunt and clean yourself up!" Although Lynn wasn't dead, she lay there motionless as if she were.

The hanging in the backyard was nobody's fault, a simple accident from us playing with the hold worn down rope that was attached to the tire swing. We had been playing with it in a jump ropeway because I was so little, and I had an extra rope that trailed behind me. "Higher!" I screamed with excitement. "Higher, higher, higher!" as I said giggling in between laughter. Lynn stood on the hillside holding onto the tree and the rope, swinging it, helping to ease the tension, or in better words slack. Then, suddenly, the extra rope that had been lying on the ground flew up and went around my neck. Lynn fell down the hillside with the rope still in her hand causing the rope to pull tight around my neck. Sadly, it looked as if Lynn deliberately was hanging me, but that wasn't the case. She was just a scared little girl who didn't realize all she had to do was let go, which would've caused me to fall to the ground. I could hear the screaming of my sister Kay calling for us to come to the house, but I couldn't speak. I tried pulling the rope off but that wasn't happening. The tension from Lynn slipping down the hillside and her weight was causing me to hang there, like the game hangman. My feet were kicking away, my face went from pale white to red as a beet. I was panicking, I could see our rundown home in the distance and Kay appearing on the porch. Then, darkness started, everything around me started to fade away, I became tunnel vision, then there was nothing, everything became black. Those faint screams were no longer there, my body was growing dimmer, and my head collapsed, as I took what I believed was my last breath.

Mother came over to Kay as she was still holding me, rocking me on her lap. "This is just fucking great, the first night of fucking bowling league and this shit fucking happens, just fucking great!" Mother said annoyed. "Just go bowling, I'll watch the girls," Kay whispered as she held onto me with tears streaming down her face. Mother looked down at us, it was then she saw the rope burn around my neck from being hanged. The rope burns were caused by the friction of the rope rubbing against my skin, causing my neck to have ligature marks. The marks were already turning brown and red. Off to the right side, you could see a blister starting to appear that was accumulating water and heaving up. "Kay, put cold compresses on her neck and give her baby aspirin. I don't have time for this shit with these two." Mother said. "I heard you the first time. "Kay stated with an irritated tone of voice. "Whatever Kay, it's always about you!" Mother said in a pissed-off tone. Mother walked out the door slamming it behind her and shaking the picture off the wall.

Kay carried me over to Lynn, "Hey, you okay Lynn? Can you move? What can I do?" Kay said with her voice cracking and tears coming down her face. "Lynn, get up, let's get your cleaned up. Come on now, she reached out rubbing her shoulder, sliding her hand down to her elbow, and gently pulling on her to encourage her to stand. Lynn, still shaking uncontrollably, finally stood up in a hunched position holding onto her ribs and walked slowly into the bathroom. She stood there looking at herself in the mirror and washing her face off, that Kay handed her. As she looked down into the lime green sink, she noticed a crimson color, it was her blood. There was blood clinging to the sides of the sink, causing the soap scum to look jarring with already-existent corrosion. "It'll be ok Lynn. I'm so sorry. I don't know what else to say. I'm just so sorry this happened to you." Kay whispered as she stroked Lynn's hair back behind her ears. Lynn just stared at her, still sobbing, and shaking uncontrollably. Kay went to put me down, but I wasn't having it. I just wanted my big sister. She almost always knew just what to do. There were ten almost 11 years between us, but she took the role more of a mother figure than of a sister. As she was stroking Lynn's hair, she was standing there rocking me back and forth, shortly thereafter I fell asleep.

That night was a long, sobering, and quiet evening. Kay sat on the couch with her arm around Lynn, her head resting on Kay's shoulder, and I was still on her lap as she held me, having my head on her other shoulder. We sat in almost silence, not knowing what to say.

Mother came in about 9:30 PM that evening, with the biggest smile on her face. "Kay, guess what? I didn't do too bad at bowling considering it was my first practice. I bowled 155 in my first game, 138 in my second, and 143 in my last game. It's going to be a great session; I just know it." Kay looked up and nodded to Mother. "That's great she said." in a less than convincing voice. "What's wrong with you Kay?" Mother said in a peeved voice. "What's wrong with me? I've sat at the house all night taking care of the girls while you bowled. I had two little girls that were almost inconsolable. Mother said nothing but rolled her eyes and walked away. "That's what's wrong with me," Kay said. Kay gathered us girls and walked into the bedroom. Here Lynn you could lay in bed with me tonight. Lynn moved over next to the wall covering up with the pink blanket. She laid me next to Lynn, a then Kay lay on the outside of the bed, closest to the door. Lynn, whispered, "Kay, thank you." "For what," Kay asked. "Letting me sleep in your bed, you never do," Lynn said. "You're welcome, now close your eyes and go to sleep." Kay said.

Chapter Four

Halloween Party of 1986

IT WAS KAY'S SENIOR YEAR IN 1986, and she couldn't be happier to move out once she graduated. She was counting down the days, literally. She was moving and there was nothing that mother and father could do to hold her back. First, though she had to get through her senior year and the rest would be history.

Kay did everything possible just to stay away from home and honestly who would blame her? She played the trumpet in high school, the best damn band around as we would say, Jewett-Scio Vikings. She had one of the higher rankings, being able to play the silver trumpet. She was so proud of her accomplishments as she should have been. She was even a member of the honored band where they got to travel.

Kay was an excellent softball player playing all positions, but mainly outfield. She tried keeping as much of a normal life outside of the home as possible, including being a social butterfly.

When she wasn't playing, she would babysit the local community kids. I lost track of all the kids she would watch. She would always make sure to watch them at their thoughts. It was the best way to be away from home and get out of chaos. It was also a way of giving me interaction with kids my age.

Luckily for her though the band practice field and softball fields were both close enough to walk mother and father had the mentality of figuring out how to get there because we won't be taking you. Walking became the new thing to those practices regardless of how hot or cold those days might have been. It was just over a mile one way, which typically wouldn't be an issue, however the local dairy farm trucks and semis would fly on that road. I can't tell you how many times we almost got hit walking to those practices.

26

Now, imagine being Kay trotting a 6-year-old and 14-year-old at hand. You guessed wherever Kay we had to go we had to go as well. Kay was their live-in babysitter. I felt bad for Kay. No matter what, she always had us girls. She was more of a mother to me than our mother.

There was a bright light though, Kay started dating an amazing young man Butchie at the end of her junior year. He was such a kind young man. Butchie was a very tall, redhead, with a contagious smile, and the best personality. From time to time when he'd visited Kay, he would run through the hallway with me and throw me onto mother and father's bed, he'd do this a few times, and each time he would cause belly laughs. Those would be borrowed and cherished times I had with him. Kay started to have a brighter smile, laughter, and an even better outlook on life. Butchie was Kay's light in the darkness that played throughout her young life. For the first time, Kay was enjoying life just a little bit more.

It was during that time that mother and father's attitudes started to change for the better if there were such a thing. If there was one thing for sure he'd never allow anyone to hurt, her. I'm not sure if that's the reason why their attitudes changed or the fact Kay was older, graduating, and they knew they had two other victims left behind. Remember I said some though.

At the end of football season, it also meant the end of the band unless you played in the winter concerts. Kay decided to ask mother and father if she could have a Halloween party, with a bonfire, and a haunted walking trail that would go up into the woods. I overheard them talking to her and telling her that she was only allowed a few friends, no more than twenty.

The day came and preparations for the party. Butch was there helping get the firewood amongst other stuff.

Kay and some friends were in the woods where her haunted trail was going to be racking leaves, making a pathway, and hanging old toys from the trees trying to create a spooky atmosphere. The smell of fall was in the air, with a hint of musty, earthy, and decomposing leaves that fell to the ground. The leaves were in full colors of orange, red, yellow, and brown, being almost the perfect postcard picture. Father's junk vehicles had the perfect scary effect at night especially, never knowing what might pop around the corner of them.

Father was stacking firewood and preparing it for that night's events where our old garden once was. As he was stacking, he smashed his finger which then caused chaos once more. "Mother fucker!" Father screamed. Kay yelled, "What happened? Are you okay?" "Fuck no, I'm not okay. If it weren't for your fucking party, I wouldn't have smashed my fucking finger! You stupid fucking bitch!" "I'm sorry father!" Kay stated.

Kay stood there frozen and for the first time her friends, I believe, caught a glimpse at how bad our home life was. They didn't know what to say, other than, it would be okay. It was then that Kay, felt the warm embrace of Butchie wrapping his long arms around her from behind. "Kay, I've got you," Butchie said. Kay turned around and collapsed into his arms. "I can't do this anymore. I just can't." Kay whispered. "Can't do what?" Butchie and the rest of her friends asked. Kay never answered, she just kept shaking her head.

Despite the blow-up that happened with Father the party was everything Kay had hoped for. She went as a scarecrow dressed in jeans with her knees cut out, a blue checkered top, and her hair pulled up into a ponytail, with a straw sticking out of her pigtails. Butchie went as a matching scarecrow they looked adorable if I must say for myself.

The eerie night was about to take place as cars started to pull in. Kay's friends started to arrive, dressed in all sorts of different costumes, even creative homemade outfits. From werewolves to monsters, vampires, and eighty's rock stars, and Ghostbusters.

An eerie feeling could be felt all over the countryside that day. Maybe it was due to the fact it was Halloween or even the costumes that the teens were wearing. The countryside transformed into a haunted wonderland with pumpkins other kids were able to bring to outline the haunted trail, and old baby dolls hung from trees putting an extra creepy feel to the already spooky land. Fake spiderwebs draped crossed weeping tree branches. It was as if you were stepping into a whole new dimension.

Something was captivating about the sight of the bonfire that frightful night, as ghosts and ghouls gathered around the centerpiece of the party. The smell of freshly burning wood filled the crisp, fall, night. The orange glow from the fire illuminated as far as the eyes could see. The stars were dancing in the midnight sky.

Ghost stories, laughter, and filled the air. The sound of dry leaves rustling as people walked amongst each other. The occasional howl could be heard as the kids were screaming at each other on the haunted trail. It was overall the best Halloween party any of the town's teens put on that year.

As Kay and her friends were sitting around the bonfire, it was finally Kay's turn to tell a scary story. "It's your turn, Kay, do you have a scary story to tell?" The kids said in excitement. The kids leaned in so they could hear her meek voice over the blaring music and laughter. "Yeah, I have one to tell," Kay said. "Well, go on. Let's hear it!" The kids said once more.

Kay began to speak her voice cracking, "Louder!" Someone said. Kay cleared her voice. "There once was a happy little girl, it was just her mother and her. Then, her mother met an amazing man or so they thought, with a little girl of his own. He was everything that the little girl's mother dreamed of. As the weeks went by, they decided to marry on one October day. The mood of the stepfather changed drastically, he went from happy to a raging, ticking, time bomb. Then, one day while the little girl's mother was away, she was left alone with her stepfather. He asked her to come to the bedroom then decided to start touching the little girl. She screamed and was then backhanded. Saying that if she did that one more time, he would kill her mother. So, she complied with what he wanted to do. Even though she knew it wasn't right of him. He had her sit beside him and grab his penis and jerk him off." Kay said before being interrupted. "Jesus, Christ Kay, what kind of fucked up story is that?" One kid said. Her friend Mel said, "Kay, what the fuck dude, that's fucked up?"

Kay had her head down and tears began to flow. Butchie wrapped his arms around her tight, not knowing what to say.

Another friend piped in, "Kay, is someone hurting you?" "No, no, it was just a story that I took too far. I'm sorry guys. Someone turns up the radio and let's get this party started!" Kay screamed, which shocked her friends being she is normally so soft-spoken.

Some of her friends looked completely shocked at what they heard. Others could be heard whispering, saying if they wondered if it was a true story. After, all why would you get so upset over a story if it weren't true?" Another whispered.

Father and mother stayed in the trailer until later that evening when they noticed well over twenty friends showed up. They stopped counting over 150 vehicles and running out of places to park, people had to start parking in the fields below the house. The music was blaring so loudly that I'm sure the neighbors could hear. This went on into the early morning hours. I'm surprised Father didn't say anything but that would come soon enough.

Father stood over top of Kay like a snarling wild animal with rabies as she lay in bed asleep. "I thought we told you twenty friends! Who the fuck were all of those people last night?" Kay jumped out of bed. "I'm sorry father. I didn't realize other kids told people about the party. I only invited twenty, in fact, 17. I had no clue all of those kids were coming. It won't happen again. I'm so sorry. It won't happen again." Kay said as her voice cracked. "You're God damn right it won't happen," Father screamed. He began to swing the yellow whiffle ball bat from head to toe. The more Kay moved the harder and longer the beating took place. He swung that bat like he was auditioning for the major league. Swing after swing!

Then finally he threw her down on the bed and began to brutally rape her. You could hear her muffled screams throughout that ratty trailer. Instead of a mother helping her, she chose to turn the radio up.

I ran into the living room where Mother sat in her red recliner, smoking her nasty cigarette, as she blew it out the window. She caught me out of the corner of her eye. "What are you staring at you little bitch?" "Nothing mother. Good morning." I whispered. "Good morning? There's nothing good about it." Mother said as she continued to smoke and blow it out the window with a blank stare.

Chapter Five

Thanksgiving What's Much to Be Thankful For

THANKSGIVING BREAK STARTED tomorrow but for us girls, you can only imagine just how joyful they were, said nobody ever. For most families, Thanksgiving was a celebration of gratitude, family, friendship, and different things to be thankful for. While most would wake up to the smell of a turkey baking in the oven from the night before. We would wake up to a bowl of cereal not saying that's a bad thing, being half the time there was little to no food in the house. All our holidays and summer vacations were the worst. When most kids were cheering as the final countdown began before the ball rang for the holidays, not me. I learned at a young age that nothing good even happens when we're out of school. NOTHING! The final bell rang to line up for the bus at the end of the day.

Sitting on the bus since I was one of the younger riders I sat in the fourth seat up, then Lynn was a few seats behind me, and Kay was able to ride with the cool kids in the back. I can't speak for them but I will say that I wasn't fond of the bus rides. Kids made fun of me calling me Trailer Trash and Junkyard Girl. To say I was embarrassed would be an understatement. I would quickly get on and off the bus in hopes that nobody would truly look around at the yard that was in disarray from the junk vehicles and scrap metal that was scattered throughout the yard.

As Kay, Lynn, and I were walking towards the trailer, Kay said, "I've got a secret!" Both Lynn and I looked at her puzzled, "Oh, yeah what's that?" "You'll both have to wait till we get inside to see. Mother and father were gone, not quite sure where they were. Once we got inside the trailer Kay said, "Go put your duffle bags away and I'll show you the surprise." Lynn and I looked at each other smiling from ear to ear. "I wonder what it could be Lynn," I said. "I'm not sure, hurry!" Lynn said with excitement. We ran into the bedroom dropping our duffle bags on the bed and ran back out to the living room.

"What's the surprise, Kay?" We both said excitedly. "Well, come here girls," Kay said. We ran into the kitchen where Kay stood over the kitchen sink. Our eyes became wide open with excitement. "Wow, where did you get that Kay!" Lynn yelled. "I bought it with my money from babysitting," Kay said. I stood there amazed, excited, not knowing what to say. I wondered if this was how the other kids felt when they saw their turkey on Thanksgiving Eve. Either way, I couldn't wait to dig into it. "Well, aren't you going to say something, Trisha?" Kay asked. "Oh, man. Oh, man. OH, MAN! It's going to be a real feast! I can't wait. Yippy!" I yelled. I felt like Charlie from the movie Willy Wonka and the Chocolate Factory when he won the golden ticket. I was so excited and filled with joy.

"Alright girls well this bird won't cook itself." Kay said. We washed our hands and found the biggest pot we had. "Now, what Kay?" Lynn asked. "Well, I've never baked a turkey before. What's the instructions say?" Kay asked. Lynn just stood there. "Move over Lynn, I'll read them." As Kay was reading over the directions her face went from excited to sad, then tears welled up in her eyes. "What's the matter Kay?" Lynn said. The turkey is frozen, it won't have enough time to dethaw. "Dethaw what is that?" Lynn and I both said. "It means to unfreeze." "It will be okay Kay." Lynn said. "I hope so." Kay said. "It will have faith." Lynn said. "I've got an idea. I'll put the turkey in the oven on low and just cook it overnight. We'll be able to have a real Thanksgiving dinner." Kay said. Lynn and I both jumped up and down with joy.

Kay took off the wrapping of the turkey and placed it in the pan. She placed the oven on 250 so it would slowly cook overnight. She didn't leave out all of the fixings either, she bought potatoes to make homemade mashed potatoes, corn, and noodles. She was so happy that she could feed our family. I hadn't seen her that happy, except for when Butchie was around.

It was late when Mother and Father made their way home that night. Their headlights illuminated the driveway and onto the side of the house. Kay looked out the window and saw that they were home. "Okay, girls remember what I said to say when they got home," Kay said. "Yes!" Lynn and I both said. We could hear the keys jingling at the doorknob, as the door crept open there, we stood just like we practiced. "SURPRISE!!" We all shouted. "Surprise?" Mother and father said. "Yes, go look in the oven," Kay said. They looked at each other in a sense of confusion. Father said, "Go ahead and open in Candy." "No, you open it, Randy." Mother said in a joking voice. We looked at each other without saying a word, surprised that they had been in such a good mood. Finally, Father opened the oven up. "A turkey! Where did you get that?" Father said. I saved money up from babysitting and wanted to surprise everyone with a Thanksgiving dinner." Kay said happily. Mother and father looked at each other surprised and smiled. "Thank you, Kay. It looks great!" Mother said. "I put it on low so it will bake throughout the night. I picked up corn, potatoes, and noodles as well." Kay said with a smile. "A real Thanksgiving feasts," Father said.

"Girls don't forget that we're going to Gram's tomorrow for dinner. So please try to find something decent to wear." Mother said. "Going down there, huh?" Father mumbled. "Yes, Randy the girls and I go every year to Thanksgiving and Christmas you know that. You've always been invited, but you chose not to go." Mother said. "Yeah, I know. I get it." Father said.

"Okay, girls get ready for bed we've got a long day ahead of us tomorrow." Mother said. "Night Father. Night mother. "I should get to bed early anyways I want to get up and make dinner so Father could have some before we go to Gram and Pap's. Plus, Ann and Peter are coming to their house to pick me up later tomorrow night so I can have Thanksgiving dinner with Butchie." Kay said. "Oh, Kay, thank you for buying Thanksgiving dinner." Mother said. "Yes, thank you," Father said.

As we lay there through the night, my mouth was watering most of the night as I could smell the turkey baking. I thought to myself of a real Thanksgiving dinner at our home like normal kids our age. We never had Thanksgiving dinner at our house before. Mother always said we would have dinner at Gram and Pap's house with the rest of the family. We've always done that.

Thanksgiving dinner at Gram and Pap's house was always amazing. You could smell the freshly baked pies, turkey, and my aunt's famous Hungarian stuffing. Her home simply smelled heavenly. She'd always have her main table where the adults would sit and the children's table where all of us kids would sit. She'd make sure that the tables were decorated just perfectly before everyone could eat. The television would always have the Macy's Thanksgiving Day Parade playing in the living room. My cousins, aunts, and uncles would travel near and far for the holiday. Aunt Gale would make the couple-hour drive from Sandusky along with her son Clarence. Uncle James would also make his way home for the day. He was one of my favorite uncles, he'd always call me "Pipsqueak." Gram always did her absolute best to make Thanksgiving special for all of us. We'd sit around the tables saying what we were thankful for, but each year I would always say the same thing, "I was thankful for the food we were about the eat and most importantly Gram and Pap." Once we were done eating, we'd have our choice of dessert, then it would be followed by the guys watching football, my cousins and I playing games, and my aunts and Gram in the kitchen cleaning. When we were there, we didn't have to worry about being yelled at. There was plenty of food to eat and a variety of it. Everyone laughed and played games, and you could truly feel what love was and meant to Gram and Pap.

It was finally time for the moment that us girls we're waiting for, Thanksgiving Day! Kay got up early that day to make sure dinner was done early so Father had something to eat before we left. The turkey smelt delicious and a beautiful golden brown, it looked perfect. Kay made corn, mashed potatoes, and noodles just like she promised. She was so proud of herself that she beamed from self-gratification of her accomplishments.

"Well, look at that. It smells great Kay. You did a wonderful job." Mother said. "Thank you, mother. I'm going to hurry and get dressed." Kay said. "I'll let Father know that the food is done." Mother said. "No, need I'm standing right here," Father said. "Well, women make me a plate," Father said.

Kay was standing in the bathroom, which was a cross from the back door. She was curling her hair and doing makeup. She had picked out a yellow button-up shirt, blue jeans that she rolled at the bottom, and her canvas white shoes. She truly was one of the most beautiful girls I ever knew, I don't think she even realized it.

Just as Kay was finishing, she heard her father scream, "What the fuck is this shit? It's the fucking giblets she forgot to take out the fucking giblets and neck before she baked it." Kay stood in the bathroom holding onto her curling iron with tears rolling down her face as she could hear the heavy footsteps of her father coming closer. He slammed the door open, almost hitting her. Kay jumped and immediately started shaking. "You left the fucking giblets and the neck inside the turkey Kay. You ruined the fucking dinner." Father screamed. "I'm...." Kay started to say she was sorry, but her father interrupted her. "Let me guess you're fucking sorry? I'll show you sorry Kay." Father screamed. He stomped off into the other room and came back holding the turkey that Kay worked so hard to make. That's when he did the unthinkable, he threw the turkey out the backdoor. "NO," Kay's knees hit the ground as she kept repeating over and over again, NO!" It was then that Lynn and I were coming out of my bedroom. Their father stood with the backdoor open and the turkey lying on the ground. I could hear Kay sobbing in the bathroom. As father stood there motionless. It was then he looked up the hallway and saw Lynn and I peering down the hallway. "What in the fuck are you little bitches looking at? See the turkey outside? Kay forgot to the giblets and neck out before baking the turkey. You all better fucking eat well at your precious Gram and Pap's house because that was the only food we had. Make sure you thank your sister here for fucking up Thanksgiving dinner." Father screamed.

There it went I thought, our first Thanksgiving dinner at home gone as fast as it was brought in. I sat on the couch unable to move, just tears streaming down my face. Lynn sat beside me doing the same. Mother came in from being outside just then. "What are you both crying about?" Mother asked. We were so upset we couldn't speak. It was then that Father came around the corner and Kay followed, "Oh you know Kay ruined dinner she forgot to take out the giblets and neck." Father screamed. Kay stood behind father with her head down, sobbing uncontrollably. "I'm sorry!" she whispered." Mother looked visibly shaken and said, "It will be okay Kay. I'll just remove them. The turkey should be fine to eat." Kay just stood there shaking her head. "You can't." Kay finally said. "What do you mean I can't?" Mother said. It was just then that she looked over at the stove where the turkey once sat and saw it was gone. "Where is the turkey at?" Mother yelled. "Ask Kay!" Father screamed. In between trying to catch her breath, Kay said, "It's outside. Father threw it outside." "I could've fixed the problem, Randy you didn't have to go and do that fucking shit." Mother screamed. Kay started to walk out the door. "Where do you think you're going?" Father screamed. "I'm going to Gram and Pap's. I'll take the girls with me. We can walk." Kay said. Surprisingly, Father and Mother didn't stop us as we made our way out the door and down that long driveway.

Kay walked with her head hung lower than low that day with tears rolling down her cheeks, causing her freshly applied make-up to run. "I'm sorry girls I ruined dinner. I'm so sorry. I was just trying to make a nice Thanksgiving dinner." Kay said. "You didn't ruin dinner. How were you supposed to know that it was there? It was the first time you ever made a turkey Kay." Lynn said. I just walked and cried; you could even say my cry sounded like a howling that day. As we were walking you could hear the roar of the fighting coming from the trailer as mother and father were behind fighting. "I hope they kill each other," Lynn said. "That's terrible Lynn," Kay screamed. However, deep down inside we all thought the same.

As we approached Gram and Pap's driveway Kay attempted to fix her makeup but there was no use. Her mascara ran through her cover-up, and blushed causing smudge marks. Once we got to the door, there Aunt Gale stood, she had the most beautiful blonde hair, the best contagious smile, beautiful eyes like mother, and a stylish outfit. "Hello, there girls, come on in," she said. It was then that she saw Kay's face as she was still trying to fight back the tears. "Kay what happened?" she said. "Father threw our Thanksgiving dinner out the backdoor," Kay whispered making sure that Gram and Pap didn't hear. She didn't want to upset them. "Oh my. I'm so sorry that it happened. Why on earth would he do that?" she said. "I forgot to take out the giblets and neck," Kay said. Aunt Gale gave Kay the biggest hug, then Lynn, and then me. "Girls, go wash up and help set the kitchen table." Aunt Gale said.

It was then that we could hear a car approach, but not any car, it was father and mother. Father never came to dinner like ever what in the world would he be here for I thought. As he sped down the driveway, gravel was flying everywhere. When they reached the front of the house, it was just mother who got out. She was crying and trying to wipe away her tears before reaching the front door, but it was no use. Everyone had just heard and seen the chaos erupt as they peered out the windows and the front door.

Pap met Mother at the door and said, "When, are you going to leave the son of a bitch?" "I'm done, I'm not going back." She spoke. "Good, you and the girls can have the upstairs rooms," Pap said.

However, like many other broken promises, after dinner and once the family started to leave. I heard Mother say, "Girls, get your shoes on we're leaving. You're dad's here." "Candy, I thought you said you were done and not going back home," Pap said. "What and leave all of that?" Mother said sarcastically.

We didn't want to go, but what choice did we have? Father always said if we didn't come home, he would kill us along with anyone else who stood in his way.

Chapter Six

The Long Good-Bye

THANKSGIVING CAME AND WENT; Christmas was long gone Kay was getting ready to graduate. She and Butchie were still together and were joined at the hip. It wasn't young love with them, it was something much more. It was a whirlwind of compassion and strength, their hearts were in rhythm with each other, instinctive if you will, like two old souls dancing in the wind with each other. Their journey had just begun. It was forever that they were reaching for. Although they were young their love was genuine, it was true, and simply pure like honey. It was the type of love that would forever be talked about. He would even ride his bike from the next town over just to come to see his girl. Without a doubt, they would've been married and started their forever together.

Lynn was about to enter her junior year. I was surprised considering all the school she had missed from being in Fox Run or missing due to not being able to cover her bruises up. She at this point was keeping to herself just to get by or perhaps for her to stay alive. After, Beckie from Job and Family Services threatened Lynn with going back to Fox Run, no matter what was done, or said to Lynn just took the punches as they came and complied with what her mother and father told her to do regardless of what those demands might have been. She almost became robotic. It was very sad because although she was human, she was invisible to those around her. Especially for the jocks, and preps, they were the ones who made her life hell away from the hell she lived in at home. "Blue Lips" is what they would call her amongst other things. Her blue lips were due to her failing heart. When she was born one of the valves in her heart needed to be replaced so the doctors used part of the pig valve to help repair the damage to her heart. She was required to take medication for it, but after a while, I'm not even sure if she took it on a regardless basis. I questioned whether she deliberately forgot to take her meds so her heart would give out and she would go in peace to the Promised Land or if she simply forgot.

Up until this point, Kay pretty much stayed away from the house as much as possible, having study groups, for her finals. Plus, she was still babysitting the community kids saving up money for college in the fall. Or being at Butchie's house visiting him and his family.

Finally, the day came when Kay was graduating. I was so young I wasn't sure what graduation was or even meant. All I knew was there was a fight that morning. When mother and father had woken up Kay was packing her clothes and belongings, putting them in boxes and bags. "Where do you think you're going Kay?" Mother said. "Well, I'm moving out once my graduation ceremony's over!" Kay stated with authority. "NO, you're not!" Mother screamed. "Look I graduate today. I'm 18 now and there's nothing you can do about it." Kay insisted. Mother began to grab Kay's belongings as Kay was packing. "Stop, this right now! I said you're not going anywhere! Kay stop! You're all, I have Kay. What will I do once you're gone?" Mother screamed and started sobbing. However, Kay wasn't giving in nor was she falling for her narcissistic tactics. "Kay I'll change is that what you want?" Mother asked while wiping tears from her face. Kay finally spun around and looked Mother in the eyes and said, "You knew I was graduating. You knew I was moving out and going to Aunt Gale's. You also knew I was planning on going to college in the fall. You can't keep me here forever and continue to be your living-in babysitter! I'm moving TODAY and that's final!" "NO! Kay, please don't!" Mother said one last pathetic plea that did not do a bit of good. Kay started to walk away and then turned around and said, "I'm going to Gram and Pap's. I want to spend time with her before I leave. God only knows when I'll be back home again."

Kay stood there for the first time in her life with confidence. Her posture was strong, tall, and centered. It was like she shifted overnight from the person she was shy, and meek, soft-spoken, to this confident run-way model who wasn't allowing anything to stop her. Who was this new Kay and what did she do to the old Kay? I'm not sure of the answer besides, she simply had enough of the chaos, confusion, abuse, and was leaving. She was my hero and didn't even know it.

There was so much confusion about the day was Kay moving out and never coming home. All I know is that she was the only mother I truly had growing up. She did everything with me even though it took away time for herself. I was practically thrown on her as a newborn when she was only 11 years old. She took care of me night and day, through bottle feedings, and changing diapers. Our house was a fend for yourself and pray for a good outcome. As you can tell though, some make it out, whereas others will have to fight for their lives.

When Kay came back later that day from visiting Gram and Pap's when she opened the door our mother sat in her red chair, smoking her nasty cigarettes, and blowing the smoke out the window. Part of me would like to think she did that because of my serve asthma, but the other part of me knew better than she even remotely cared. I don't believe a woman like a mother is truly capable of loving because she doesn't even love herself. I'm not sure if she even did or would.

"Hello, mother, how are you doing?" Kay asked as she sat on the couch. "Oh, you know grand, you're moving out, one less mouth to feed, and one less bitch in the house." Mother said sarcastically. The tears on that woman seemed to happen naturally like a water faucet with a turn-on and shut-off valve. She continued to puff on her nasty cigarette and blow it out the window. Although the mother was never diagnosed legally for being a narcissist, I believe the definition fits her to a T! She would have highs and lows, self-gloat about how important she was almost put herself up on a pedestal of high admiration for herself. However, back in the 80s and 90s narcissistic personality disorder was finally getting diagnosed in the States, but mother would never be diagnosed. "Well, we talked about this and knew I was moving to Aunt Gale's. Now, are you and Aunt Tillie still driving me to Sandusky? Or should I make other arrangements to get there?" Kay asked. "I'll fucking take you, Kay!" Mother screamed. "Alright then. I'm going to finish packing and then get ready for graduation." Kay said with excitement. As she was getting off the couch the phone rang. "I'll get it," Kay said. "I'm sure you will." Mother said. "If you're not home you're on the phone." Mother mumbled. "Oh, mother it's for you. It's Gram." Kay said.

Kay was packing when Lynn and I came into our bedroom. "Whatcha, doing Kay?" I went over and sat on the bed staring at her with tears in my eyes. "Where are you going, Kay?" Lynn said. "Well, girls I graduate today from high school. After that mother and Aunt Tillie will be driving me to stay with Aunt Gale in Sandusky. Lynn and I both burst into tears. "You mean to tell me you won't be living with us Kay?" Lynn said. I couldn't breathe when I heard the news, our saving Grace, our big sister, was moving out. She took a lot of the abuse for us, by sticking up for us for the most part. "Hey, now wipe those tears away," Kay said as she was wiping away tears from her own eyes. "Lynn, I need you to do me a favor," Kay said. "What's that Kay?" Lynn whimpered as she was still wiping tears away. "I want you to watch over Trisha, while I'm away at Aunt Gale's and college. Can you do that Lynn?" Kay asked. "You want me to watch over Trisha?" Lynn asked puzzled. "Yes, and Trisha you watch over Lynn," Kay said. We looked at each other and said, "Yes, we can do that." "Promise?" Kay said. "We promise." We both said.

Kay's graduation went off without a hit or so I thought. It was years later we found out that the mother had run into Kay's biological father in the hallway of the school just outside of the gymnasium. Mother was going to the bathroom with me when she stopped dead in her tracks, motionless as if she saw something she was uncertain of what she was looking at. Then, talking through her teeth she said, "Kenny, what are you doing here?" She locked eyes with Kenny, staring at him with the evilest half-ass grin, her body stiffened, as if she were going to attack him like some wild animal. Finally, Kenny said, "I'm here to see my daughter graduate Candy. Why else would I be here?" "LEAVE RIGHT NOW!" Mother said as she was grinding her teeth together. "I'm not going anywhere. We're staying to watch our daughter graduate." Kenny said. "We?" Mother said. It was then that petite women looked around this Kenny guy's side. "Why, hello Candy. How are you doing?" "Carol, you are fucking bitch you don't need to be here to watch MY daughter graduate." Mother snapped. "Candy, enough. It's a public building. We're staying and there's nothing you can do." Kenny said. "LEAVE RIGHT NOW KENNY and take that whore with you!" Mother said. Kenny took Carol's hand and walked off. I thought to myself Man I don't know who those two people were but their presence just irritated Mother.

We hurried to the bathroom and as I looked up at Mother she was crying. It was the type of cry as if she was about to bury a loved one. Although, I was well aware that children should be seen and not heard. I whispered, "It will be okay, mother." She glanced down as she was opening the bathroom stall, "What do you know you're just a kid?" As I was trying to pee, I jerked because it was so painful. It must have been because of Father playing house with me earlier that day.

46

"Hurry up Trisha!" Mother said. I finished up quickly because I learned a long time ago never to upset my mother or father for that matter.

We rushed back to our seats making sure not to miss Kay's ceremony starting. However, I saw Kenny and Carol sitting in the corner on the opposite side of us. Our eyes locked, but I didn't dare say a word to upset Mother any more than she was.

One by one each graduate's name was called and then it was Kay's turn. "Kay Potts will be going to college in the fall at ICM." The announcer said. Her smile was radiant that day. I thought at any moment that her smile would crack her face, that's how big it was. Off in a distance, I heard a group of people yell, "Great job Kay! We're proud of you!" I looked up into the bleachers and there was Butchie with his parents Ruthanne and Pete. When he saw me looking, he waved and smiled. I wouldn't realize until it was too late just how those small moments would impact me, even years later.

After the graduation ceremony, Kay met up with their mother, father, Gram Pap, Butchie, and his parents. They wished her all well in her future endeavors and hugged her. Butchie stood there with his arms wrapped around her. It sorts of looked funny to me being she was only five'8 and Butchie towered over her with his six'5 figure. However, Mother was on a schedule that day to get Kay to Aunt Gale's house and told Kay to "Hurry up!" in her fashionably nice tone when others were around. Kay said her goodbyes and went to walk away, but Butchie pulled Kay closer. "You promise me you'll call once you get there Kay?" Butchie whispered with tears filling his eyes. "I promise," Kay said, fighting back tears of her own. Although 2 hours isn't that far away, for two star-struck lovers who are teenagers it might as well been a million miles away. "I love you Kay Potts and don't you forever it," Butchie said. "I love you too Butchie," Kay whispered as she gave him one more tight hug before walking away. Little did they know Butchie was on borrowed time and just how precious their time together would be.

As Kay was walking towards the car you could tell that she was upset because she was wiping tears away. "Kay, are you okay?" Lynn asked. "I sure hope so," Kay whispered. From time to time, I'd look over at Kay and smile. Typically, she'd give a big smile, with an occasionally funny face. This time, she just smiled and put her head down with sadness. It was the kind of sadness as if you lost your best friend to other kids on the playground. She was still wiping tears away. Mother looked in the back seat and rolled her eyes when she saw Kay crying. "Knock it off Kay you're the one who wants to abandon your family." Mother snapped. Kay looked up and said, "You mean to earn money for college since I'm paying for it on my own?" Even with the scholarship that Kay had received to ICM in Pittsburgh, it still wasn't enough to pay for all costs. "Whatever Kay. It's always about you." Mother said. That seemed to be the famous comment to Kay although Kay never made it about her. Kay was simply stating facts. It was those facts that Mother hated.

Kay was finishing up her packing and walking her last box out to the car. Mother stood in the kitchen, leaning up against the stove, you know that stove that once had charcoal lighter fluid in it when father was trying to kill us. "Kay, I've got something to tell you. You're not leaving your family. You're not moving to Aunt Gale's. You're staying here." Mother said with a little smirk to her face. "What do you mean I'm not going to Aunt Gales? How am I supposed to save money for college?" Kay said with a panicked voice. "Well, that's simple. You're not going to college either Kay." Mother said. Kay dropped to her knees, "No, no, no, no..... Please don't do this to me. I want to go to college and better myself." Kay said in an angry voice. "Get over yourself, Kay. I was just teasing you. Take your stuff out to the car. We're running behind." Mother said. Kay glanced up, her baby blue eyes, swollen from crying, and finally said, "I can't believe you'd say that just to see my reaction." Mother didn't say a word, just looked down and started hysterically laughing.

Father had walked out of the bedroom at this point. Their bedroom slammed open, having knocked a picture off the wall in the process. You could hear the heavy footsteps coming closer to the living room. There our father stood, hair wild as can be, in his light blue work pants, his stomach protruding as if he could give birth at any time. "HEY, what the fuck is going on?" Kay stood there frozen as she was bent over picking her belongings up. Then, she stood up swung around, and said, "What the heck does it look like I'm doing? I'm packing. Like I told Mother she knew I was graduating. She knew I was going to Aunt Gale's to work and save money for college in the fall. That's what I'm doing!" Kay stood there staring at him, waiting for the next round of abuse to happen. Waiting for the next punch, the wiffle ball bat to be bounced all over her body, or even the newspaper that was wrapped in black electrical tape to hit her. She was there standing her ground for the first time again the man, who brutally raped her, beat her, starved her, manipulated, and abused her for the last 8 years of her life. It was then that for the first time, she felt that she was invincible. "Well, um." Father went to say something, but Kay pushed her way past him with a box she had in her hands. "I didn't say I was done talking to you! Get back here kid. Get your fucking ass back here, right fucking now!" Father screamed as he was walking through the living room, he punched the wall beside him causing that picture to also fall. Kay was already outside packing the car up by the time he got through the living room. He stood on the porch screaming, "You're not going fucking were. Get back here." Kay looked back right before getting into the car and yelled, continued to ignore him, and got into Aunt Tillie's car. Aunt Tillie then beeped the horn for Mother to come out. Aunt Tillie hardly ever went inside of the trailer, besides who would blame her? Finally, Mother reached the car puffing on her cigarette. "Candy put that nasty thing out. You're not getting into the car with it." Aunt Tillie said. "Well, isn't that fantastic? This is going to be a long ass ride." Mother snapped. "I guess so Candy. So, what was that about?" Aunt Tillie said. Without missing a beat, both Mother and Kay said, "Nothing." "Um...yeah that was convincing." Aunt Tillie said as she cleared her throat.

On the drive, they passed through Amish Country in Sugarcreek Ohio. It was a beautiful countryside stretch that led through the rolling hills of Ohio with some of the most spectacular views. Kay saw small towns like ours, to major cities, and once they got closer to Aunt Gale's house, they saw Lake Erie's Islands. Some of the best lighthouses were homed within walking distance of Kay's new house. Kay got happy when she saw Cedar Point off in the distance and the faint screams of the coaster enthusiast. It was an amazing site to see.

Once they got to Aunt Gale's it was dark. Aunt Tillie beeped the horn, allowing Aunt Gale to know they had made it. "Well, Kay, you've made it to your new home. What do you think?" Aunt Tillie asked. "It's beautiful," Kay said with amazement and shock. Not the sort of beautiful flower during the summer months. It was the sort of beauty that was breathtaking, indiscernible, and homey feeling. It was the intense feeling of knowing that Kay had a whole new life that she was about to embark upon and most importantly she'd be safe from the clenches of abuse. As they were pulling into the driveway, Kay thought about her freedom and how she wouldn't be going through all the abuse like she once was. Tears began to flow, but these weren't any ordinary tears, from pain, frustration, sadness, and anxiety. These were tears of happiness, which was a rare feeling, but a very overpowering feeling of freedom that Kay's never felt before.

Aunt Gale came from the backside of the house. Although Aunt Gales was Mother's sister, she chose to stay in the car as Kay began to unlock. Aunt Tillie got out reaching Aunt Gale before she was ever close to arm's length to hug her. "How are you doing?" Aunt Gale asked mother. "I'm okay. It's so hard to believe that it seemed that Kay was born yesterday and now she's moving in with you, then college bound. I'm not sure where the years have gone. I guess I blinked." Mother said. "Yes, they grow up that's for sure. She'll do great here. Stop worrying." Aunt Gale said as she leaned towards Mother and rubbed her hand to reassure her. "I know but I'm going to miss my girl." Mother said. "Miss her girl? She didn't let me feel this way the whole time while living at home. She made my life a living hell. Even allowing her husband to do the things he did. Kay thought to herself. "Candy, why don't you get out and visit?" Aunt Gale insisted but it did her no good. "No, we've got to get home before it gets too much later, especially with the 2-hour drive." Mother said. "Yes, Gale sadly we both have a hard time driving and I've got places to go first thing in the morning." Aunt Tillie stated. "Well alright then." Aunt Gale said with disappointment. "Well, I hate goodbyes Gale you know this, so we're going to go since Kay has all of her stuff unpacked." Mother said. "Candy why don't you get out and give Kay a hug?" Aunt Tillie insisted. "No, I just said I don't do well with goodbyes." Mother said. "Just tell Kay I'll see her in a couple of weeks." Mother said as they were pulling out of the driveway.

Kay was coming around the corner from taking the last of her belongings in the house when she saw the taillights pulling out of the driveway and Aunt Gale waving goodbye. Kay stood there beside Aunt Gale which startled her. "Oh, Geesh, I didn't see you standing there Kay." Kay began to laugh, then quickly said, "I'm sorry." "Oh, honey that's not your fault." Aunt Gale said and she raised her hand to push back her hair, but Kay flinched. "Why did you just flinch? I wasn't going to hit you." Aunt Gale said. "I'm sorry," Kay said as they were now going into her new home.

Aunt Gale her views were spectacular Lake Erie in the front part of their house just crossed the roadway, and the bay behind her house. Their boathouse sat just off to the side of the back of the house. The house had multiple bedrooms, a catwalk leading to each room, with a spiral staircase. It was nothing like our house where you'd have to wear shoes just to keep your feet remotely clean. There at Aunt Gales, your shoes came off at the door, the soft carpet lay just perfectly between your toes, and the smell of a freshly burning candle filled the air. Kay, after over 8 years, was free of the madness she once experienced.

Kay, grab your stuff and I'll show you your room. As Kay was walking behind Aunt Gale, she couldn't get over the huge bay window that covered both stories of the house allowing natural light in. "Well, Kay here it is. What do you think?" Aunt Gale asked with excitement. "It's beautiful. I love it." Kay said with a shocked face and a look of disbelief. The carpet felt amazing between her toes, and you didn't have to wear shoes in Aunt Gale's house you had to take them off so the carpet wouldn't get dirty. "Well, go on Kay put your stuff down. You can have those two dressers for your clothes and closet. Through those doors is your bathroom too." Aunt Gale said. "Wait, I get my bathroom in my bedroom?" Kay said with excitement. Aunt Gale laughed at the enthusiasm Kay had,

"Yes, sweetheart you get your bathroom. Now finish putting your clothes away." Aunt Gale said.

My bathroom, my bedroom, I don't have to wear shoes in the house to keep my feet clean, and best of all I'm away from mother and father. Then, a rush of sadness came across Kay, she thought about Lynn and me and the guilt of leaving us behind. Tears began to swell in her eyes once more and she wiped them away. Aunt Gale turned around and saw Kay crying and gave her a soft smile. "Homesick already Kay. I know it will be hard, but you'll manage." She spoke. "No, not at all just sad that I left my sisters behind," Kay said. "I understand." Aunt Gale said.

The following day Kay started working at Cedar Point and before she knew it, a few weeks had passed by. It was the day she was anticipating. Mother and father were bringing Butchie up for her to see. As Kay was walking down the spiral staircase, she couldn't help but smile. "Look at your smile, Kay! You looked wonderful." Aunt Gale said. "Thank you so much I just can't wait to see Butchie. I've missed him so much." Kay said. "Well, they aren't the only ones coming up Kay, what about your mother and father?" Aunt Gale asked. Kay just stood there, with a blank look on her face. "Well, I'm going to grab cereal before they get here. Do you want me to make you a bowl?" Kay said. "Sure, that would be a great sweetheart." Aunt Gale said.

Just as Kay and Aunt Gale were finishing up breakfast, they heard a car pull into the drive. Kay jumped up with excitement and ran to the door. "Butchie's here! They made it." Kay yelled. She opened the door and ran to Butchie, there he stood stretching his long legs out. "Butchie, Kay screamed, just as he turned around, she threw herself onto him, jumping into his arms and wrapping her legs around his waist. "Oh my God, you're here! I missed you so much Butchie." Kay yelled, then leaned in and gave him the biggest kiss. "I love and miss you too Kay," Butchie said. "Enough, enough, nobody wants to see this." Mother yelled. "Then, go somewhere else," Kay said as she continued to hold Butchie tight. Mother took a deep breath and mumbled something as she walked towards the house with father following close behind. "Hello Candy, welcome Randy." Aunt Gale said. "Hello Gale," they both said in an almost rehearsed tone of voice. "Where's the girls Candy?" Aunt Gale asked.

It was a great day at Cedar Point for Butchie and Kay. They rode rides, ate amazing food, and laughed. Their young love was truly one of a kind which nothing could ever replace. When they were around each other, nobody else existed, even in an amusement park filled with thousands of people. Their whirlwind love was so beautiful and rare, one from a storybook. It was at Cedar Point that Butchie gave Kay a small engagement ring, it was nothing spectacular, but to her it was everything. Knowing how mother and father would react they chose not to tell them, just keeping it between her, Butchie, and his parents. They didn't want to bother with the extra stress of telling everyone, so they'd have to hear how young they were and how they shouldn't marry till later in life. Even though Butchie still had a year left of high school and Kay had 4 years of college once she started. They were smart enough to wait till after they both graduated from college and got their future planned out.

The time came that Mother, Father, and Butchie had to make their way home. It was like a punch to Kay's gut, she didn't want to let him go, like something told her that something was about to happen. After, they said their goodbyes instead of Kay going back into the house she walked to the bench that was in the back of the house to decompress before walking back into the house. Walking was something that she would do a lot to clear her mind of the chaos around us when mother and father would fight or even worse when father would playhouse with Kay. It wasn't long after she sat down that she heard Aunt Gale, "Kay you okay sweetheart?" she said. Kay couldn't speak, she just shook her head back and forth. "Long distance relationships are hard Kay, especially for young couples like yourself and Butchie. It will be okay." Aunt Gale said. They sat in silence, but Aunt Gale didn't leave her side, she put her arm around Kay telling her that it would be okay. This is something that Kay wasn't used to. We never had reassurance from our mother and father. They would just yell at us, calling us babies, or asking the famous question, what the fuck is wrong with you. Not Aunt Gale, she was so kind, a saint if you will. Once Kay calmed down, she went to bed after crying herself to sleep that night still with a sickening feeling in the pit of her stomach.

It was late when the trio came home that night. I was so excited to see the headlights coming up the driveway that night, Butchie was getting out of the car and carrying something. I ran to the couch pretending that I was asleep, ha-shhhhh, ha-shhhhh, ha-shhhhh, I was saying with my fake snore. I wasn't fooling anyone that. Then, I heard Butchie say, "Well, I guess you can take me home since Trisha's sleeping there. I wouldn't want to wake her up. I'll wait to give her the surprise later. "SURPRISE! I jumped up excitedly. Where's my surprise Butchie, huh?" "Well, there you are. I didn't want to wake you up sleepy head." Butchie said. "Ha, ha, I gotcha Butchie." Well, I suppose you did." Well, here you go, Trisha. I won you a basketball today." Butchie said. "Thank you Butchie, I love it." "Alright, I've got to go home. It's been a long day." Butchie said. I jumped up all excited, "Before you go can you pick me up?" He used to pick me up so I could touch the ceiling. I always felt like I was on top of the world. He was so tall. He'd also take his two fingers in the middle and pointer and pick me that way. He had so much fun. He was one of a kind and God for certainly broke the mold when he was born. As he was walking away getting ready to leave, he said "Bye squirt." Butchie said. "Bye, Butchie". I said excitedly with a wave.

That was the last goodbye I would ever hear. He tragically passed away two days later in a horrible car accident. Although he was Kay's boyfriend, he brought light to the madness of our house. When he was around his mother and father acted like they weren't the monsters they truly were.

It was late at night when Mother answered the phone, "Hello, yes, Ruthann. Is everything ok?" Mother asked. It was then that I heard the most blood-curling scream I had ever heard in my entire life. I ran back to my mother and father's bedroom when I got there. There our mother sat on her knees rocking back and forth, screaming, "No, not Butchie. Not Butchie." Mother screamed. It was then that my young self-caught onto what happened, "Is Butchie, ok, mother?" I whispered as I put my hand on her shoulder. "NO," she screamed. It was then the first time in a long time. She grabbed my hand and brought it down to her lap. She sat there rocking with me as we both sat there crying together.

Mother called Kay and only got the words out, "Butchie, gone, Kay. Butchie's gone." The faint screams could be heard over the phone of Kay, screaming. Mother called Kay and only got the words out, "Butchie, gone, Kay. Butchie's gone." The faint screams could be heard over the phone of Kay, screaming till she could scream no more.

Kay was beyond devastated as anyone would be. I questioned if she would go on to college during the fall. She blamed herself for the longest time, not sure if she ever truly mended from his passing. He was the light of her life in so many ways, now he watches over her.

We endured so much loss, so much devastation, and heartache as children. I'm not too sure how we survived, but we did. Butchie ironically enough passed away June 20, 1987, and I was writing this chapter the day before the 37th anniversary of his death. It just goes to show the impact that he has had on all our lives. He was one of a kind and will forever be loved.

Chapter Seven

More Than Money Was Stolen

IMPATIENTLY WAITING FOR THE CLOCK to start at 2:30 PM to hear the last bell of the day for the school to be let out. That day seemed to take forever, I'd look up at the clock thinking that an hour or two passed only to be disappointed with only 5 or 10 minutes passing since the last time I anxiously checked. Besides, when you're 7-years-old being in school for the day it can feel like a lifetime. Ms. Longville yelled, "Put your pencils down! Time's up! Pass your test forward." That day we had a test on cursive, we had written A-F capital and lower case. I looked around the classroom and everyone was busy passing their test up front except one student who always seemed to be mean as a snake. There she sat, our eyes locked, I tried to quickly look away but that didn't help. She sat in her seat sticking out her tongue and putting her hands up to her ears and waving them back and forth. Her eyes crossed and then she placed her thumb up to her nose, bending it backward, making a pig nose, then pig sounds. Just then she was midway through making a pig nose and she must have inhaled her spit and began to start coughing uncontrollably. "Rebecca, what are you doing sweetheart? Are you okay?" Ms. Longville asked. Shaking her end in between coughing she answered with a yes. Her face turned as red as her hair and finally, she settled down. She looked almost embarrassed.

She was always nice to the other boys and girls except me and one other boy who smelled like a combination of salami and coal from their fireplace. His family was like mine, poor and simply trying to make ends meet. More so than not he would wear the same clothes as the day prior and sometimes could come to school in the same shirt for three days in a row. David would wear an old hoodie with dark blue and white stripes, his pocket was torn at the corner, so it was very easy to tell it was the same hoodie. His same pants were obvious as well with the knees blown out along with his black canvas shoes that had a hole in his right shoe so badly you could see his socks. His sandy blond hair seemed to have a greasy glow to it and his brown eyes seemed worn out considering someone of our age.

She'd teased us and went as far as putting my gum in my hair. Luckily, she moved mid-school year. However, when she left off, her friends picked up. I could honestly say I hated school, even going as far as having anxiety. My heart would race from the time I got there, till the last bell.

Lunch that day was pizza, those were my favorite days. I made sure to clean up my tray. I was extra hungry since the night before mother didn't make anything to eat. I never wanted to say anything, because I didn't want her or father to feel bad, but on those days, it was hard to fall asleep and my little stomach would sometimes make grumbling noises throughout my bedroom. I'd resort to drinking water if it got too bad. It was those sleepless nights that made going to school the next day worth it, at least I'd have breakfast and lunch, which would be guaranteed. However, I would fall asleep in class a lot of times which caused me to visit the principal and get paddled. The paddle was long with holes in it, which caused the paddling to be worse. I hated those visits; it was bad enough that I would get paddled at home with the yellow wiffle ball bat, or the rolled-up newspaper that was covered in black electric tape, the nearest shoe, or an object that was close by. One time I remember mother throwing her shoes at me and when that wasn't good enough, she picked the wiffle bat up beating me from head to toe. I never meant to be bad, but sometimes I couldn't sit still, I was hyper, distracted easily, couldn't focus, and stayed on task like the other kids. It's like my brain would go a thousand which ways, but hardly focus on the task at hand.

Finally, the alarm went off. It was 2:30 PM, we anxiously stood up, cleared our desks off, and pushed our chairs in to get ready for the next day. The walkers would be called to stand in line first since they were the group of kids who walked to school. One by one our bus numbers would be called so we could be dismissed to get in line and wait for the big yellow bird to pull up to take us back home. As my bus number was called, I threw my bookbag over my shoulders making sure to snap it, so it didn't fall. It was then that my strap snapped causing the bookbag to be uneven, collapsing to the side. Shoot I thought, mother and father are going to be angry with me. I began to get nervous and sick to my stomach for what was about to happen when I got home. I should have been more careful. I should have paid attention. I shouldn't have shoved so much into my bookbag. What I was thinking was all my fault. Maybe they won't notice. Then, the idea hit me, I could get into my mother's sewing material and find a needle and thread, and I could sew it back myself. That's exactly what I'll do. They won't even notice it once I'm done. The only problem is I've never seen it before. Then, I heard Rebecca say, "Look, her family's so poor, they can't even afford a nice bookbag like the rest of us can. Some of the kids erupted with laughter. "Ha, ha, ha, look at her! She's so poor she lives in a tin can." one boy named Alex said. Another boy named Kevin stated, "They're so poor they live in a rundown shake. "Trailer trash, trailer trash, trailer trash," Jason exclaimed. Then, a few others joined in the taunting. "Trailer trash, trailer trash." "Enough class!" Ms. Longville said. As I looked up with tears in my eyes, I noticed the slight smirk that came from her lips. It was almost like she was approving of the class's behavior. I felt so alone in this world already, but to have a teacher join in on the tactics was even worse.

Tomorrow will be a better day as I walked through the hallway, thinking to myself. I brushed my hair back out of my face and as I reached the steps, I noticed the principal, Mr. Howard, standing at the bottom of the stairs. He looked up and smiled as our eyes connected. "Have a good day, Trisha," he said. "You too, Mr. Howard," I said in between sniffling. Darn, I hope I'm not catching a cold; I thought as I pushed the double doors open. As I made the turn to get in line for the bus, their father stood with Lynn next to him. Lynn was leaning up against the fence and her ankles crossed. Her hair was blown on each side and the back teased with so much Aqua Net it looked like it was cemented to her head. Her jeans were bleached from her mother trying to accomplish the latest style. Her off-the-shoulder shirt hung loosely, her dirty bra strap visibly showing, and her pink rocker-style glove on her left hand.

Father had his blue work pants on and long-sleeved matching top. Although he was a jack of all trades, not having a regular 9am-5pm job, mother found several matching pants and tops at a yard sale. Kay was already in college just starting that fall in Pittsburgh. He wore them daily, so he always looked like he was wearing the same clothes.

"Hello, father and Lynn." I said with a slight smile. They both looked like they were nodding and said, "Hello". "I thought I was supposed to ride the bus?" I said subconsciously almost in a pouting manner. Not that the bus was any better. I hated having people know where I lived. Father had junk vehicles scattered throughout the yard, a small shed off to the left side with trash and junk that lined our driveway. It was never organized; it was always in disarray. The kids would make fun of me calling me "Trailer Trash" or "Junkyard Girl". I swear there was never a dual moment if I wasn't getting into trouble at home and being yelled at, I was getting yelled at during school, and the kids would make fun of me. It was a never-ending cycle.

As we approached the car, I noticed that mother wasn't inside. Lynn sat beside father in the passenger side seat in the Cutlas and I jumped in the back seat. As father was driving, he kept clearing his voice. I thought how odd, he only did that when he was upset or about to scream. I sat there in silence listening to the oldie's music.

Then, before, we reached the only red light in our small town of less than three hundred people. Father cleared his voice one last time as if he was about to scream. The next thing I saw was his head going down and back up, looking at the road straight ahead of him. Then, he said, "Girls, I have something to tell you." It was almost in a whisper, like he was uncertain, second-guessing himself.

We looked at him puzzled; we hardly ever saw father like this. He was either screaming, beating someone's ass, or not home. There was no truly happy medium with him.

"Your mother won't be home for a while." he finally said. "Where's she at, I could make dinner tonight, so she doesn't have to. Do we have Salsberry steak? I could make that and potatoes." Lynn said. "How late will she be a father? Is she bowling tonight for the league?" I asked. "No, she got into trouble today at work," Father said. Lynn looked over at their father, "When is she coming home? What sort of trouble? What did she do?" Lynn asked almost as if she was a detective, trying to get to the bottom of the crime. All she needed was a trench jacket, a magnifying glass, and a bloodhound to sniff out the bad guys. However, the bad guy was our mother. "She was arrested today for stealing from work. I don't know all the details. Just that the cops showed up at her work and arrested her for stealing." Father said. "What do you mean, stealing?

What did she steal?" Lynn asked as her voice began to crackle then tears started falling from her dark brown eyes. "She stole money, merchandise, like toys, watches, and a bike. Now, you fucking know what!" Father said in a snarling voice. The year prior mother started working at Schrader's Tire in the office. They sold car tires, toys, watches, bikes, and other sorts of electronics. It was nice because she'd bring home an array of the latest styles of watches, and toys, and I even got a new bike once. Little did we all realize those generous gifts were stolen for her work. I always questioned subconsciously where my mother was getting the money being there were nights when I went to bed hungry. Maybe she just didn't feel like cooking those nights or we were just that poor. All I knew was there no food offered and I was too young to cook. Lynn began to cry and then I started crying. "Now, what did she have to go and do that for?" I said out loud. Typically, I'd get in trouble voicing my opinion. I'd always be told children should be seen and not heard by their fathers all the time. I was never really allowed to speak unless spoken to. I sat there looking out the window for the rest of the trip home, watching the trees go by and the cows the local farms had on our road. We passed Gram's house and my Aunt Tessa and Uncle Pete's house being we were all neighbors, then we pulled into our driveway. You could hear the dogs barking in the distance. Crystal was our Afghan hound, she was beautiful with long grey hair, we had she lived all her life tied up on the hillside till one day she disappeared and never came back. Then, Inch-High, my sister named her that because she was the rut of the litter and inch high to a grasshopper. She was a black lab with the most beautiful golden-colored eyes. Then, of course, Lady, the dachshund that Father had before marrying Mother, was the only dog allowed to be inside beside Mac. He was the other dachshund that was brown and black, he was blind, so he'd run into the couch on occasion. We also had only one cat, he was old and named Pusser who was orange like Garfield.

I made sure when I got out of the car that day that to tuck my broken strap so father couldn't see it. Walking to the trailer, you could smell the rain in the area, it seemed that a thunderstorm was brewing over the hillside, but that wasn't the only thing brewing. We stood in silence on the porch as Father bent over to pick the key that was hanging under the porch. Let out a grunt as he was getting up. We all walked in almost quiet like a church mouse, not knowing what to say, or do. The house seemed colder than usual that day, the smell was stale, almost no smell at all, and the dust was starting to collect on the boxed T.V. Mother wasn't much of a cleaner. Lynn stood there looking around I'm going to start cleaning; it was almost like she could read my mind and how I was thinking how dusty the house looked. "Trisha, go put your bookbag down in the bedroom and come help me make dinner. While dinner is cooking, we'll do some cleaning." Lynn said in a humbling voice. Lynn and Kay were the ones who were always in charge of keeping the house clean. If they didn't do it, the house would be dirty,

As we stood in the kitchen, getting ready to make Saulsberry steak and potatoes. I looked at Lynn and said, "She's not coming back, is she?" I asked. Lynn looked down, I couldn't tell if she was upset, happy, or scared, perhaps a little bit of all three. She said with a half grin, "I sure as hell hope not!" I was taken aback because I had never heard Lynn talk like this before. "Now, get into the deep freezer and get one box of Saulsberry steak out and open it up, poke some holes in it with a fork," Lynn said in an almost demanding voice. I did as she said and thought to myself mother was always so mean to Lynn, making her do the housework, except for the clothes mother always washed and dried, but had one of us girl's fold, she would have fed and watered the animals too. There wasn't much that Lynn didn't have to do. At one point my grandmother who was my father's mom, called Kay a bitch just like mother, I was a monster, and Lynn reminded her of Cinderella because she was always cleaning and tending to mother and father's needs. Lynn stood over the sink washing off the last three potatoes.

Father called Kay while we were making dinner, it was a short conversation. I can't say I blame Kay. After she graduated in May she left the same day and moved to Aunt Gale's house on Lake Erie so she could work at Cedar Point and save money for college in the fall. She was attending a college in Pittsburg for business management and had received a few scholarships to help pay for the expenses. She was on her way to move mountains and had a fresh start. I'd even say, a fresh start to freedom. I was so proud of her for getting out while she could. Kay must've answered because I heard father say, "Yeah, your mothers in jail for stealing. I just thought I'd let you know." Right after they hung up. He was motionless when he was talking to her, no facial expression, no I love you, nothing. It was a very cut-and-dry conversation. They never got alone much. However, she'd get the occasional t-shirt and get to attend a concert with him. It was years later that I'd find out that never came without a price to pay. It was a price we all eventually had to pay, some of us sooner than later.

Once dinner was done, I was too tired from all the crying that I had done, which seemed to be the new norm. Lynn and her father were watching T.V. Which I thought was odd because we always had a bedtime, 9 PM SHARP no excuses. As I lay there, I could hear laughter coming from the living room, although it didn't last long, I just kept thinking how odd. As I was lying in bed the room was pitched black, except for the glow of the bathroom light coming through the hallway. There was nothing on the walls, I didn't have an ordinary bedroom like most kids. We were poor, barely getting by.

Sometime that night I woke up to noises. I often heard those types of noises coming from the bedroom when mother was home or when their friends the Dawson's were over. I never heard it whenever it was just Lynn and I, with Mother being at the bowling league. I got up making sure that I was quiet not to wake Lynn. We shared a bedroom, she slept on the top bunk because she was a big girl, and I was on the bottom. One day I'll have the top bunk like a big girl, one day. I made sure to open the door as quietly as possible and walked down the hallway. The bathroom was next to my bedroom, then my mother and father's bedroom. I noticed that their bedroom door was cracked open, barely enough for me to press my face up against the door to see what the noises were. There Lynn lay on her back and her father was on top of her. She lay there with a blank look on her face, almost too scared to move, as she lay there looking off to the right side where Father's closet was. She must've seen me peering into the bedroom because she let out a scream, "Trisha, what are you doing?" Father jumped up, and there he stood fully naked, with no clothes on. I ran down the hallway, maybe if I got to my bed I could lay there and they'd think I didn't see them, playing mother and father games? I hurried and covered up, pressing my body against the wall, and throwing my blankets over my head so only my eyes could be seen. There, they'll never know what I thought. Almost as soon as I thought that the door creaked open. There, father stood, naked. I couldn't move, I couldn't breathe, my body began to tremble all over, my teeth began to chatter. "I know you're awake, kid, get up." Father said. I couldn't though, I lay stiff as a board. Father walked over, "Get up, get your fucking ass up right now." he yelled. He pulled me from bed, then grabbed me by my neck, and shoved me back to their bedroom. I stood there shaking, not knowing what was about to happen. I didn't want to know what was about to happen. I wanted to run, but I was too scared too. Lynn was crying lying in bed. "Please, don't hurt her, she's just a little girl. Leave her alone, here you can have me. Come back over here father." Lynn said. No matter what Lynn said, there, father stood, and then suddenly, he threw me onto the bed. Lynn grabbed me, holding onto me. She was trying to protect me, but my father wasn't having it. He slapped Lynn, then screamed, "Put her down, she wanted to be a nosey little bitch. Now, I'm going to show her what a nosey little bitch gets." Lynn, come to daddy." Father said. It was then that I cringed, I remembered about that day in the truck when I went to the coal mine and he had a surprise for me, it was the day he had me play with his hotdog. I began to panic, "NO, NO, NO, please don't, I'm sorry, I'm sorry, I won't get up again. I'll go back to bed like a good little girl. See I'll go to bed now." I jumped to my feet and grabbed for the door. It was then that Father erupted and screamed, "You're not going anywhere you little bitch." He grabbed me by my hair and threw me back to the bed. Lynn by this time was standing, almost hovering in the bedroom corner. I looked over at her with the most helpless face, a defeated face. Father got into bed. I tried like hell to get away, but he wasn't having it. He grabbed me by my head and jerked it closer to him, his hot dog to be exact. "Suck it you little bitch, suck it," Father demanded. I had no clue what I was doing, but I knew his hot dog was in my mouth and I didn't like it. Lynn stood in the corner screaming and begging Father to stop. He didn't stop. That night never seemed to end. That was the night my childhood was robbed of me. I just wouldn't know anytime soon; just how much was robbed until later in life.

Chapter Eight

Easter Was Not So Happening

MONTHS AFTER THE MOTHER WAS ARRESTED for embezzlement from Schrader's Tire she was released on good behavior. If only that judge and the right people realized just how she was maybe she wouldn't have gotten released. Maybe they would have thrown the key away forever. However, all those maybes, all those moments of wishing for both mother and father to be put away for a lifetime, would never happen.

As I was sitting in Ms. Laughlin's class, I heard the loudspeaker come on, which got my attention from my boring assignment. "Trisha McAfee to the office, Trisha McAfee to the office please!" Mr. Howard announced. What in the world did I do now? I don't want to get the paddle again. I sat there and got tears in my eyes. I promise I'm a good girl, I'm just misunderstood. I don't mean to come to school and fall asleep, I'm just so tired because my father has been insistent that Lynn and I sleep in his room with him. We've been sleeping in there since Mother got into trouble. Why did she get into trouble? Why did she have to do that to us? I hope she's happy with herself. I got up sliding my chair in and I couldn't hold my tears in any longer. As I looked around the classroom, I heard Jessica say, "I wonder what she did now?" "Who knows!" another stated. I couldn't handle it anymore, I looked back at both and said, "Shut, up!   What do you know anyways!" Ms. Laughlin tried stopping me and I walked past her, grabbing the door and slamming it behind me.

On the walk to the office, I thought why can't everyone leave me alone? I'm not a bad little girl. I'd be better if I just could get some sleep maybe at night so I'm not falling asleep in class, maybe my grades would be better. Man, there sure were a lot of maybes flying through my brain.

I went to reach the doorknob and caught the profile of my father standing there. What does he want? I didn't want to open the door. I didn't want to hear what he had to say. I simply didn't want to be around him. He must've seen me because he opened the door just as I was about to push on it. Without looking at him, I gave my attention to Macy the secretary. Hello Macy, I'm here. My voice cracked. Do I have to see Mr. Howard for something? Macy smiled, causing her glasses to be pushed back onto her nose further. Her yellow shirt highlighted her beautiful green eyes. "No, your dad is here to pick you up! Get your coat and belongings." Still not making eye contact with Father, I turned around and started back up to my classroom.

I opened the door not making eye contact with anyone and walked straight to the closet room to get my jacket and bookbag. I was impressed with the bookbag still holding up after I had to sew it so Father wouldn't see what had happened. As I walked out of the closet room, struggling to toss the bookbag around my other shoulder. I ran right into Ms. Laughlin. "I'm so sorry, I didn't see you there," I whispered. The look of defeat and despair must've been written all over my face that day. Ms. Laughlin knelt in front of me; she had an almost sad expression on her face. Her brown curly mullet hairstyle reached just below her neckline. Her dress was a green and red plaid, with darker black stockings, and black shoes. "Trisha, are you okay? Where are you going?" she asked. "I'll be okay, as I was still struggling with my book bag." Here let me help you with that. She reached over and placed my other strap across my shoulder. Just as she was doing that, she must've noticed the scar from me being hung. "What happened Trisha?" Ms. Laughlin said. "Oh, that's nothing," I whispered, trying not to disturb the rest of the class all the while pulling my shirt past the mark. "Trisha, I've noticed you've been struggling to stay awake in class, it's affecting your grades. Should I call your mother or father to have a meeting?" Ms.

71

Laughlin said. "NO, please don't do that. I'll try to get my grades up. I promise." I said panic-stricken. "Well, once you get back from Easter break, we'll have to crack down on it if you want to pass," she said. "I whipped away the tears that began to form, looked at her, and smiled. "Deal I promise!" "Okay, but you're giving up your recess," she said. I shook my head okay. "Alright, now get going. Enjoy your Easter break," she said with a smile.

Father was standing at the bottom of the steps leaning up against the wall. "Are you ready? What took so long?" Father said. I didn't dare tell him that I'd been so tired from playing "House" at night that I was behind on my school assignments more than usual. So that day I lied and said I was finishing up a test. After all, I've been working hard on being a good girl. I didn't want to disappoint him. He reached for the double doors, and opening them, the Cutlas were parked in the first parking spot just outside the doors. I opened the back door because Lynn was also with father. He must've picked her up first I thought.

Father drove almost all the way home; then finally said "I have a surprise for you both. "What is this surprise you speak of?" Lynn asked as her voice cracked with nervousness. I didn't say anything, but I was scared like Lynn was to find out what this surprise was. See sometimes Father would get us out of school so we could play, "House." I don't think I want to know what this surprise is. I thought as I stared at the back seat till we got home. "Trisha, will you please help me clean the house? There's not much to do, but the trash, and help with the chores tonight?" Lynn asked as she investigated the backseat and winked at me. "Yes, I can do that," I whispered. As Father was pulling up into the drive he said, "That's not necessary girls." It made me sick to hear those words. I knew what Lynn wanted to do was try to protect us from playing "House." Now what are we going to do? I don't want to playhouse."

Father walked several steps ahead of us on that sandstone pathway. Lynn, I don't want to playhouse. I don't want to." "Then, don't," she said. How do I get away with this? "Say your stomach hurts, go to the bathroom, and pretend that you're throwing up. Don't forget to make noises like you're throwing up." Lynn said in a rushed manner as we were about to go inside the house.

Lynn went first, and I trailed behind her. I tossed my book bag up on the flowered loveseat. Lynn started to head to the bathroom. Then we heard, "Girls where do you think you're going?" I turned around and their mother stood in the kitchen. Her oval shape was now not so oval, she lost weight. Her hair was a little longer and for the first time in a long time, she had no make-up on. Prison for embezzlement sure did have a makeover on Mother, but not sure if it was for the good or not. She was released from prison roughly 9 months after being arrested. Come to find out she had been pocking the money for some time. It wasn't getting spent on us girls, for food or clean clothes. I'm not sure where the money went but after so many years, I imagine it went to her. Mother was indeed one of the most selfish and narcissistic people I would ever grow up to know. It would take me years of torment and questioning myself about the rights and wrongs of life before I would realize that I was just a little girl, a little girl who was groomed to be something she wasn't. We stood there frozen, not knowing what to do. We looked at each other dumbfounded. Then, Lynn ran over to their mother and hugged her, merely knocking her over. Lynn began to whale as she was hugging her mother. Mother looked up, tears coming from her eyes. "It's okay Lynn. It's okay Lynn. Lynn breathed, she almost sounded like she was hyperventilating. Lynn, it's okay. I'm home now. I'm home now Lynn." Mother said.

I stood there at the loveseat still frozen, not wanting to move. I didn't want mother to touch me. I didn't want to touch her. This lady called herself a mother. A mother would never leave her children behind. A mother would never have done the stuff she'd done. Then Father stood behind me, "Go hug your mother. What's wrong with you? GO!" Father said in an agitated voice. I walked over in a not-so-convincing way and wrapped my arms around Lynn who was still clinging to Mother for dear life. Then, it hit me, Lynn and I won't have to playhouse anymore. Mother's home so she can do it. I burst into tears and let out a huge sigh of relief. We were free, we were finally free. I could get my bed back; Lynn could lay in her old bed. This will be a new start, a new beginning. I was overwhelmed with emotions by now. I can't believe we were free. "I love you, Lynn," I whispered. "I love you, too Trisha," Lynn said as she sniffled from the tears.

"Well, doesn't this call for a celebration?" Father said. "Yes, it does, it sure does." Mother said. "Girls, go get decent clothes on we're going to the buffet in Steubenville," Father said. Decent clothes, what exactly are decent clothes to them, since the mother was gone most of my clothes were either stained or simply not washed. Lynn was too scared to wash them except hand washing in the sink for fear she'd ruin the washer and dryer. The last thing she needed was to get into trouble. Father has a temper like no other and when he was set off it was hard to calm him down. We couldn't. We just let him say or do what he had to do so we didn't get into any more trouble. I can't count on my hands and toes how many times he threatened to kill us because there wouldn't be enough space. He was a ticking time bomb. I found a pair of jeans that had a hole in the knee and the knee and a blue top that almost didn't fit me, but it was the best one that I had, really nothing else. Lynn wore a black sweater, with a V-neck, her black jeans, and black shoes. She was really into black these days. In all fairness, it went great with her olive skin.

During the drive to Steubenville mother and father were talking about how things were going to be better this time and how nothing was going to separate them again. I sat in silence and then tapped Lynn. She looked over and I rolled my eyes at her, and finally went cross-eyed! Lynn and I busted up laughing. It was the wrong time and place to do so. Our calm drive turned into a nightmare. "What the fuck is so funny?" Father said. I looked at Lynn and grabbed her hand tight. "I'm sorry Father, I was trying to be funny, by making a face. It won't happen again." I whispered. "I'm sorry father. We were just trying to have fun." Lynn said. "Fun, huh, you're just trying to have fun?" Father yelled. "Randy, please slow down. Don't do this. Not today. We're supposed to be celebrating. Please don't do this, slow down." Mother said in a calm reassuring voice. However, that didn't help nor was the father having it because the more the mother said to slow down the faster the father went. I held onto Lynn's hand even tighter.

That was the day I thought we were going to die. He kept speeding, just when we thought there was no end in sight. There was a siren, a cop to be exact. Father pulled off to the side of the road. He looked in the backseat, "See what you did." Father said angrily. The cop got out of his car, stopped at the rear of the car looked at the license plate, then came over to the driver's side, he tapped on the window with his flashlight. "You seem to be in a hurry there sir. You were going 90 in a 55. What's the reason? Is there an emergency?" the cop asked. "Why, yes sir, you see my girl has a heart condition and she wasn't feeling well," Father said. Lynn and I looked at each other puzzled, but not saying a word. "A heart condition.

What's wrong with her?" the cops said. "Her heart is racing. We're on the way to the hospital." Mother chimed in. "Okay, well put your hazards on and I'll alert the department that you're on your way to the hospital with your daughter. I hope she starts to feel better. You have a good night, sir." the cop said and walked back to his car. Father pulled back onto the highway. "Now you little bitches will be getting your asses beat when you get home. Guaranteed you that shit!" mother said. Well, isn't that nice I thought one minute father and mother were talking about new beginnings, but some things don't change.

We got to the restaurant we sat there eating, almost gorging ourselves. It's been so long since we've had a decent meal. I mean Lynn did good while mother was away, but she only knew how to cook those T.V. dinners, mashed potatoes, hotdogs, macaroni and cheese, and lunch-meat sandwiches. I had cake, mashed potatoes, roast beef, and shrimp. It was one of the best buffets around in the eighties. Lynn sat beside me. She was quiet. I'm not sure what she was thinking at that moment, but she sat there twirling her noodles and barely eating. I wonder often what she was thinking, maybe I could've helped her along the way. If I only knew how to help her. If at such a young age, I had known how precious time would be with her I would have spent more time with her.

Our bedtime came and went since we didn't get home till after 10 pm that night. As mother stated earlier, she didn't forget about her promise. As we were brushing our teeth and getting ready for bed, I heard mother scream, "Get out here right now and line up!" Lynn stood up as straight as a soldier and I put my head down while brushing my teeth. "I don't want to go out there Trisha. I don't want to do this again. I don't want to live like this." Lynn said. We walked through the hallway to the living room and bent over the kitchen table.

Mother followed shortly after, carrying the yellow wiffle ball bat. I was the first one she beat me from my shoulders to the tops of my ankles. I stood bent over making sure not to move or I would get it more. It was poor Lynn's turn. She was already crying and already having a hard time breathing. Mother started on her shoulders, moving down the small of her back, and just kept beating her repeatedly. I didn't count, it happened too many times. "Miss me?" mother shouted. "Yes, mother, I missed you. I missed you mother. I love you, mother." Lynn said. I'm not quite sure why Mother hated her so much. Maybe it was because Lynn was from father's second wife father had full custody of Lynn when father and mother had met. Mother was the only mother Lynn ever knew. You would have thought Mother would have taken her and treated her the way she treated Kay. Kay was from mother's first marriage, the love of her life. At least that's what I heard her call him when I overheard her talking to someone on the phone. Lynn just wanted to be loved, accepted, and treated right. That's all. I stood there thinking how unfair this was, we were just trying to have fun. I guess I should have known better because after all children should be seen and not heard.

Lynn and I went to bed, hardly able to walk, not able to talk from us both hyperventilating from being so undone from what Mother did to us. We crawled into bed, trying to find the right position to lay in. The sting from the yellow wiffle ball bat is indescribable. It's like several beestings, but worse. Although a wiffle ball bat is a lightweight plastic bat, it would leave an almost u-shaped bruise if any bruises were left, along with red marks from being hit so hard.

Mother and father would make sure to beat us in areas where you couldn't see our skin, typically the back, the buttocks, and legs during the winter or colder months. During the spring and summer, they were sure just to leave it between the shoulders and buttocks area. They were slick with their abuse and anyone who had the slightest suspicions would say, "Oh, well with Lynn's condition she bruises easily, or you know our girls they like to play rough. My favorite one the whammy of all, they must've fallen." Playing dumb and convincing people was easy for them. They were both well-liked within the community. Although it was controversial when they first started dating. You see she was raised with money and most of her side of the family were well established, brokers, real estate agents, and business owners. Whereas father's side was not wealthy at all, they would haul trash, and junk cars, and lived on welfare. However, when father and mother met it was due to her tire being flat, he changed it. So, the rest was history. I just wish Mother knew what she was getting into, but I wouldn't be here if she hadn't met him that day. Nor would my brothers who were born too early for life before me. They would've been my only biological siblings, but God had better plans for them to live free of the chaos that bestowed upon our hold.

The following morning it was so hard to move, I woke up stiff, my body just aching from the night prior. I lay there looking around and finally decided to get up. Getting dressed that morning was a treat for less words. I noticed how badly bruised my legs and buttocks were. I didn't want to show Lynn what kind of sister I would be to complain to her, being she got the shit beat out of her. I hadn't seen Mother that angry since the time she dragged Lynn across the porch and into the house for accidentally hanging me. It was never clear that she didn't do that on purpose. Every time I would attempt to say anything I was always asked, "Am I speaking to you?" Of course, my answer would be the same, "no." Then I would either walk away or go play.

It was Easter Eve; I had been anticipating this since the year prior. For a 7-year-old that could feel like an eternity.

Typically, one of the only traditions mothers did for any holiday was to color the eggs, we'd get a small basket of candy, and if we were lucky enough a toy or two.

Mother had just made a spaghetti and French bread dinner. The smell of spaghetti and French bread filled the air, you could smell the garlic that Mother used. "Dinner's done come to get a plate." Mother yelled. Mother stood there making everyone's plate, which was odd. We sat down getting ready to eat, my mouth was watering, thinking about dinner. Her spaghetti was one of the best. Lynn sat across from me, Mother was off to my right side at the head of the table and Father was directly across from Mother. The pot of spaghetti was in the center of the table along with the French bread. "Alright go ahead and eat." Mother said. As I was cutting my spaghetti getting ready to take my first bite. I heard the mother scream, "What in the actual fuck! Lynn, can't you keep your fucking hair out of anything around here?" "I'm sorry mother. I didn't know." Lynn said. Their mother sat pulling Lynn's long black hair out of her mouth. "She didn't know. She didn't fucking know?" Mother screamed, her face was red and foaming at the mouth. I looked up from my plate, poor Lynn's head down, staring at her plate of food. "It won't happen again, Mother. I'm sorry." Lynn said, her voice was cracking. "Well, I'll tell you what you little bitch, you can eat all of the fucking dinner." Mother screamed. "Now, Candy, calm down. I'm sure she didn't mean it. Besides, you made dinner. What do you think the kid did pull her hair out and put in the spaghetti?" Father asked.

I was surprised Father stuck up for Lynn. He never did that for either of us for that matter. That made Mother enraged. She flipped her plate upside down then scrapped the food up and threw it inside the pot of spaghetti. She took Lynn's, mine, and father's doing the same. "Hey, I was fucking eating that,

Candy! What the fuck are you doing?" father shouted. "What the fuck do you think I'm doing? Dinner's over, it's fucking over!" Mother screamed like a raging lunatic. Lynn visibly shaking, with tears, said, "I didn't mean it. I had no clue it was there. I'm sorry." "You're sorry, you fucking cunt, you're sorry? You're going to be sorry." Mother screamed in Lynn's face. Father stood up and pulled Mother from her. "Don't do this. You've only been home since yesterday. Haven't you done enough damage?" Father shouted. "What is that supposed to mean, Randy? Huh? What exactly is that supposed to mean?" Mother screamed back in Father's face. "You were arrested, sent to prison for embezzlement, and left me with the girls," Father shouted back. "Like that's my fault?" Mother screamed back. "Who else's fault would it have been?" he shouted.

"Here Lynn, eat this! You are fucking cunt! Eat this!" Mother screamed. I was still sitting across from Lynn. So scared I didn't say anything I couldn't move, or even speak. I just kept staring at Lynn as our eyes met her beautiful brown eyes said it all. She was done. I just didn't realize how done till the next morning. It was then that mother shoved Lynn's face into the spaghetti. "EAT IT YOU BETTER EAT IT ALL OR ELSE!" Mother screamed. Lynn frantically reached for a fork; it kept fumbling over the table in front of her because she feared what might happen next. "NO, you can eat it with your fucking hands like the pig you are bitch!" Mother shouted.

There poor Lynn sat with her hands in the spaghetti bowl eating it like a damn animal. She wasn't an animal, she was a person, she was my sister, and even more so a human being. What was done to her throughout our childhood wasn't fair to her. She deserved a better life than she had living in our childhood house.

"Make sure once you eat your fucking hair since I almost did." Mother shouted. Lynn must've been getting full, when suddenly, she shouted, "I can't do this. I can't eat anymore."

Lynn was still very sick, and her childhood illness wasn't going away anytime soon. She was at least 20-30 pounds underweight from the rest of the teens her age.

"EAT IT BITCH! EAT IT!" Mother screamed in her face, causing spit to fly out of her mouth and hit Lynn. "I ca....." Lynn barely got the words out and then it happened. Lynn stood up and threw up all over the kitchen table and pot from which she was eating. I hurried up and got up from the table because I didn't want her vomiting to go all over me. "What the fuck are you doing?" Mother screamed once more. "I can't," Lynn screamed. It was then that Mother slammed poor Lynn's face into the vomit. "Now, eat it cunt!" Mother screamed.

"ENOUGH!" Father screamed. That's when father shoved mother backwards causing her to hit back on a plant stand that was by the front door. It was her prized plant, a philodendron. The stand smashed into several pieces and the plant went everywhere. "Now, look at what you did!" Mother screamed. "Look what I did? Father snarled. "Look at what you've done!" he screamed. "That's right sticking up for the cunt some more!" Mother screamed as she took the potting soil, throwing it off to the side. "Bitch, I will fucking kill you. Do you fucking hear me?" Father snapped. "Too much prison life caused you to grow some fucking balls huh?" Father screamed. "Should I remind you of who the fuck you're messing with?" father shouted.

It was then that he stepped over top of her and went to their China cabinet. There it was his pistol that we all grew too familiar with. By this time Mother was standing up, halfway between the kitchen and the living room. He grabbed her by her throat. Her hands immediately went over his. The gun, better known as "Pistol Pete," was now pressed against her left temple. "I could kill you right fucking now!" It was then Father did the unthinkable he took the safety off and pulled the trigger. "BANG!" father howled from the top of his lungs. "I guess it's a good thing that I didn't reload "Pistol Pete," after I cleaned him the other day now huh?" Father said laughing hysterically. "You should've seen the look on your face."

Lynn and I were hovering in the corner of the kitchen where the refrigerator stood. She held onto me with such a tight grip that my arm was beginning to hurt. I didn't care though. Just as much as Lynn needed me during that moment, I needed her even more. I just wish I had time to tell her just how much she meant to me. If only I could have a little while longer. It was then that Father turned and saw us huddling in the corner. "Girls, get ready for bed. Lynn go shower and clean up girl." Father said in a somber voice. He almost couldn't look at Lynn, because she had vomit all over the front of her shirt, causing a putrid smell. I almost threw up myself but didn't want to eat my vomit like Lynn was forced to do so.

Later, that night I turned round and looked at the clock, it was after 4:30 am, and it was officially Easter Day. "Lynn, are you awake? PSSSSTTTT, Lynn? I'm scared Lynn, I had a nightmare. Can you come to sleep in my bed?" I whispered, sure not to wake Mother and Father. What seemed like an hour and Lynn didn't reply. "Lynn, are you awake?" I said in a louder tone of voice. Finally, I jumped out of bed and climbed up the ladder to the top bunk. I went to reach for her, but she wasn't in bed and her bed was made. I jumped back down and went to the bathroom thinking she was using it, but she wasn't there. I went to the living room, and I could see clear into the kitchen, Lynn was not there either. Maybe I missed her. May she need fresh air and was sitting on the porch. I opened the door and peered out, but Lynn wasn't there either. I ran back to our bedroom and double-checked this time I climbed into Lynn's bed. She was gone.

It was then I had to walk down that long hallway to my mother and father's room. I didn't want to wake them. I had no other choice though. I reached for the bedroom handle, opening it up slowly, their mother and father lay sound asleep. I was scared to wake them for fear of what might come next. I didn't have a choice in the matter. "Mother, father, are you awake?" I whispered. Mother almost jumped from the bed. "What's wrong Trisha?" Why aren't you in bed?" she whispered trying not to wake Father, but that was a little too late for that. He sat up in bed. "What's wrong Theresa?" Father said. My whole life he called me Threasa not Trisha because he couldn't pronounce my name right. "I'm scared, Lynn's not in bed. I had a nightmare and was going to have her climb in bed with me." I said as tears streamed down my face. "What do you mean she's not there?" Mother and father said at the same time. "She's gone." They both knocked me over as they ran past me to see where Lynn was. I indeed was telling the truth. She was gone. Lynn ran away from home.

Chapter Nine

Coming Home

LYNN WAS SENT AWAY FOR HER TACTICS of running away Easter Eve and was sent to Fox Run a juvenile detention center and spent all of spring and most of the summer there. It was a children's home for "problem" children under the age of eighteen. I was never allowed to visit Lynn while she was away. I'm not sure if it was because of my age or the simple fact stories would get compared. There were always ways of covering up the abuse by blaming Lynn's condition and her bruising so easily. Or going as far as saying it was self-inflicted for Lynn to get attention. Those were all lies, bald-faced lies. It simply amazed me that mother and father were the problem, but she's the one who got sent away. For the longest time, I sat back and scratched my head about it. Until years later when I simply realized it's all about who you know and who you blew. It was nothing but politics. Father was great friends with the sheriff at the department, Mother had her connections to resources. It was a never-ending cycle of Lynn running away then mother and father convincing the sheriff's department and Department of Job and Family Services that it was Lynn because she was a troubled child, but never them. Their narcissistic attitudes always came out on top. Then poor Lynn would be brought home in the clenches of her abusers.

Kay was mainly abused by their father who took her virginity at a very young age. She was around 10 years old when her mother and father married, and Lynn was 7 years old. Mother and father would always describe us as his, hers, and ours. My twin brothers were born in November of 1978. However, they couldn't be saved due to not having the technology that they have today. Mother fell pregnant with me at the end of December 1978, and I was born the following September. I was their official rainbow baby and last child. I was often compared to the boys having statements thrown in my face like, "You shouldn't be here. If the boys lived, you wouldn't be here. My favorite of all times, I wish you were dead, at least if the boys were here, you wouldn't be causing us problems." mother would always say when she got on her tangents.

The day mother and father picked Lynn up from Fox Run I was sent to stay at my Gram and Pap at their house.

Driving down her long driveway you could hear the gravel hitting the underside of the car. There was a small sandstone bridge that you had to be cautious to drive over because it was extremely old and not in the best shape. Her oak trees lined the driveway reminding me of the classic southern-style homes without the sweeping moss. Her jasmine tree that was across from the house had the sweetest smell in the spring and parts of the summer months. Its aroma would change throughout the season from a little to a heavier sweet touch to an almost musky filling of the air. It could smelt while swinging on her large porch. Sometimes I'd even climb under it through the foliage entrance and underneath. There were days I even fell asleep under it. It was one of the best locations, the view was always breathtaking regardless of the season. Cornfields were all around their house, making hide and seek some of the best times. The smell of cow manure could be smelt all around. I'd even go as far as smelling it in the next town over. Weird enough, it is one of my favorite smells. It's a country girl thing that I wouldn't expect a city person to ever understand. In the warmer months, Gram would hang her hummingbird feeders up and we'd sit outside on her swing or chairs watching the hummers fly by. They'd go as far as to dive-bomb us, causing on a few occasions people to jump or scream because they got so close. I always thought that was the funniest thing ever.

Her house was a beautiful farmhouse with a red barn off to the side. Her hanging baskets on her front porch hung just right. Her green outdoor carpet matched her shutters perfectly. She had one dog; his name was Jock, who wasn't the friendly character. He was a white, small poodle that both Gram and Pap loved dearly. During Thanksgiving and Christmas dinner everyone was cautious as to where our feet were to be sure not to bump or accidentally kick him with our feet. He was all but blind and would get scared if he were bumped and would nip at your ankles or legs. Gram and Pap just loved that dog but for the rest of us, he was a walking, nipping, ticking time bomb.

As mother and father approached Gram and Pap's house, father said, "You know nothing about what's happening! As far as you know Lynn tried killing herself and that's why she went away. Do you got me, kid?" as he said talking through his teeth. "Yes, father," I whispered. I paused for a second making sure that he was done talking to me. As I opened the door, Father said, "Hey, kid you breathe a word, I will kill you." That seemed to be the common threat or promise unkept at our house. Perhaps it made him feel big in that small mind of his.

I always hated it when he talked like that. My little heart would race, my palms would get sweaty, along with my forehead, and it would make me feel anxious. I learned later in life, what I was experiencing was anxiety, PTSD (post-traumatic stress disorder), and separation anxiety. All of these are mental health illnesses that are caused by the chemicals in the brain that have been changed due to environmental stress, traumatic life events, and mental, physical, or sexual abuse. Each one of us girls had this in common and struggled with it all our lives. Amongst other mental health disorders. I always thought how unfair this was, if only we lived in a loving, caring, compassionate family versus the abusive, hateful, and hurtful one we had.

I got out of the car, closing the door with ease. Father and mother always hated it when I slammed the doors shut. I learned my lesson though after the first few times just how much they hated it. One time I slammed the door. Father asked me to "get back in and the car." I did as he asked then, he asked me to do it a second time which I did as he commanded. It was then he said, "Hold on kid I have something for you and backhanded me so hard I'm pretty sure that Jesus felt the welt on his face.

As father and mother pulled out, I stood on the stoop of Gram and Pap's sidewalk waving goodbye. I often prayed they'd leave me there and forget to ever pick me up but that was never the case. I'm pretty sure they just kept me around for what was called welfare benefits. I'm not sure what mother and father did with their benefits, but there were days when there wasn't enough food in the house. We'd either go hungry or have dinner with our Gram and Pap. A lot of times Kay would make us homemade French fries from the potatoes we'd get from our garden. Those were always the best fries. They never seemed to mind those days and neither did us girls.

I made my way up her sidewalk reaching the door, there my Gram stood, "Get yourself in here, come on." She'd say with a smile. My arms would wrap around her waist, and I'd give her the biggest smile. Her hugs were always the best as she would rub my shoulders as I'd pull away. What I would do to have one more smile. One more hug. One more embrace from the women who helped make me the person I am today. "Whatcha want to do?" Gram said as I was kicking my shoes off. If there was anything she disliked, it was shoes being worn on her beautiful blue carpet. I remember one time I was so excited to see her and Pap that I ran across her floor giving him the biggest hug. She scolded me that day, but nothing like what father and mother would do. She had me sit at the kitchen table and not talk for a couple of minutes. Which was hard to do because I always loved to talk to them.

"Hello, Trisha," Pap said. "Hello, Pap. How are you feeling?" I asked. "I'm doing fine," Pap said in a weaker old man's voice. He was up in his age around 85 years old. He was tall and slender, and coke bottle glasses, with shards of little white hairs, would lay on his head. He'd always have Circus Peanuts or Orange Slices right next to his chair on their end table, with his pack of cigarettes.

I remember one time in my younger teenage years, he had fallen asleep, and I crept up beside him thinking he was asleep. I reached for his cigarettes, managing to get one out that Lynn and I split, but not before he slapped my hand as I was putting them back. "Put those down" he growled. Later, that day he looked at me and winked. I knew that he knew what my actions were that day, but he never told me. He was ornery, to say the least, but he met his match when I was born.

"Trisha, leave Pap alone and come out here, I brought some crafts out from the craft room. That day was one of the most memorable days. We sat with felt paper making a butterfly for my school project. She always amazed me with just how crafty she was. To this day I think I get her artistic flare and my drawing ability from my Aunt Gale. The butterfly was dark blue with buttons for its eyes and piping for its antennas. She was simply an amazing Gram, all the way around.

A short while later, I heard the gravel being thrown up and a cloud of dust following it as mother and father were back from picking Lynn up. I thought, "Great just what I needed. I didn't want to go home. I didn't want to go back to the one place I couldn't get away from once they got their clenches on us. I didn't want to go back and have to playhouse. I didn't want to go back to the house where I didn't feel loved. I hated it there."

Father sat outside like he always did, laying on the horn, and refusing to come to the door. He hated my grandparents along with the rest of my mother's side of the family, unless they were giving him handouts. He spent the holidays alone most of the time due to not liking, "Her snobby side of the family," as he would call them. I never did get that. That family was the only family who showed me any type of love. Yet, he was ungrateful for what they would do for us girls and them. All the holidays they would make sure that we girls would have a decent Christmas, from toys, to games, and clothes which was always my favorite. Not too often did Mother take me shopping for decent clothes. She always said they didn't have enough money. Then would make me feel bad when I told her that I needed something. She'd almost always complain that we didn't have the money, so I would stop asking. However, that didn't help either because then I'd get into trouble if I asked my grandparents. Our grandparents along with Aunt Sara and Lawson were our lifelines a lot of times. I remember on several occasions running out of fuel oil, and they would fill the tank up so we could stay warm in the winter along with paying the electric bill so we could have lights.

I threw my shoes on making sure I gathered my belongings and put them inside a grocery store bag so I could be ready when Father beeped the horn. "Thank you, Gram, for helping with my butterfly project," I said with a smile. "God-bye Pap." speaking somewhat louder he was losing his hearing. I often questioned if he was losing his hearing or if it was selective hearing. There he lay though, sound asleep in his favorite chair, his glasses almost falling off his tilted head. I immediately apologized to Gram. "I'm so sorry, I didn't know he was asleep.." I said tearfully. "What's the matter Trisha?

Why are you so upset?" Gram asked. "I don't want you mad at me," I whispered. "Oh, nonsense. Why would I get mad over that?" Gram said. "I don't know, because he was sleeping," I whispered. "Go on now there's your parents," she said.

It was just then that father beeped the horn. "Great, now I'm really in trouble." I thought. I walked quickly down to the car. There Lynn sat in the back seat. From what I could see she looked great, and even gained some weight. Her face wasn't sunken anymore. I opened up the car door glancing over at Lynn with a smile that shortly changed. She could barely look over at me as she was blowing her nose and whipping tears away. I thought to myself what is happening in the world now? Other than crying and blowing her nose she looked great.

"Hello, mother and father how was the drive?" I asked. Nobody replied and Lynn still sat there whipping her nose and drying her tears. Then, I remembered that I should've already known not to ask Mother and Father anything. Father's famous phrase then shot to mind, "Children should be seen and not heard." It was then that as I was buckling my seatbelt up I got backhanded. "Why, did you just speak?" father shouted. "I'm sorry Father it won't happen again. I was just excited to see everyone." I said whimpering in the backseat. "You're God dam right it won't," he said. I thought to myself great here we go again. I reached for Lynn's hand as I often did, but this time was the first time she pulled away. That right there broke my little heart. I sat in that musty-smelling backseat and began to wail even harder. "Dammit girl, I'm going to give you something to cry about!" He screamed.

Gram and Pap had no clue or at least that's what I'd like to believe. I truly believe they might have intervened or maybe not because of father's violent temper that we all grew acquired to seeing.

Father fishtailed as we were leaving our grandparents' house, not quite going all the way sideways, but it was close enough. Mother, let out a scream, "Randy you almost went over the bridge. Please, slow down." "Speed up? Sounds great, Candy, thanks for the suggestion." Father shouted. It was then we reached the top of Gram and Pap's drive without slowing down, without looking each way, father pulled out making a sharp right turn, causing the driver's side tire to go into the ditch. The car shook valiantly as we hit the ditch and the side of the hill. Father roared like a wild lion that day that was losing control over his cubs, "See this girl, if you were both good none of this would have happened! Wait till I get you home. He was so angry that spit was flying from his mouth hitting his beard" as he screamed, smacking his hands on the steering wheel.

Father sat there trying to get the car out from the ditch, by rocking the car back and forth. It was no use though. The tires were spinning and not getting any traction to get it unstuck. There was so much mud that it had caused the car to be unbalanced.

Luckily for us, I say this sarcastically that farmer Larry was coming up the road just then. "I see you're stuck there Randy let me help you out there." "Thank you," mother, said with a smile. "You girls alright back there? That must've caused such a scare." Larry said. "Lynn whispered, "We're ok, just shacked up, Larry," Lynn said as she was whipping the tears away.

It was then that she turned her face just slightly that I could see her left cheek with what appeared to be a handprint. It was then I knew that Lynn must've been slapped before they picked me up that day. "Are you okay, Lynn? What happened?" I said in a shaky voice. "Like you even care, Trisha. I bet it was nice being at home and having mother and father all to yourself huh?" Lynn said. I thought, "What in the world, is she even talking about? She's the one who ran away from home and let me all alone with them." Yeah, that must be it, Lynn. You don't have the slightest clue what I've been through. Shut your mouth." "Shut the fuck up Trisha, it's always about you," she said in an angry voice. "All about me?" I spoke. "Yes, all about you. Just like now, had you not spoken to us when you got in, we wouldn't be getting our asses handed to us when we get home." Lynn stated. "I'm sorry Lynn I am. I love you." I whispered because at this point my face was getting ready to get back into the car. "Whatever you little bitch." Lynn said in an angry whisper.

Father got back in the car, "What were you girls talking about how much you're going to like your asses getting beat" he said. Without missing a beat, "No Father," we both said. Mother looked back and said, "Well, you were talking about something. What was it?" Lynn chimed in. Nothing Trisha just asked how I've been doing is all." she said with a smile. "Umm, huh." Mother said with her iconic eye role.

The car began to rock hard back and forth, then about the third hard jerk, the car was free. "Thank you," both father and mother said. "That was no problem." How did you get yourself in there anyhow?" Larry asked. "Umm well, there was a raccoon in the middle of the road that I couldn't bear to hit." Father hurried up and started. "That must've been some raccoon," Larry said with a chuckle. "That it was." Mother said. "Well, okay now, I've to get back to work, it's almost feeding time," Larry said. "We'll see you later, good man," Father said with a wave and smile. Mother sat there and gave her, Miss America wave goodbye.

Nothing was said the whole way home. Mother and father got out of the Cutlas. "Hey, girls, don't forget, your father has something for you when you get into the house." I taped Lynn, "I'm sorry Lynn." I whispered so low that not even a church mouse couldn't possibly hear me. "Whatever, shut up!" Lynn whispered.

Before we even reached the steps, their father stood with his famous, yellow whiffle ball bat. He ran down the steps, I swear that day at the speed of light. Lynn and I just stood there because we knew if we ran it would be ten times worse. He started on me, because I was the one that spoke first, then went to Lynn. He beat us that day, I swear within an inch of our lives. He took that bat and smacked us on the back of our head multiple times. As it hit us you could hear the cracking sounds from the impact. He kept screaming, "When, will you two bitches finally get it that, children should be seen and not heard? Now say it God dammit. Say it!" As each one of us was taking a beating from hell, we kept repeating, "Children should be seen and not heard! Children should be seen and not heard. Children should be seen and not heard." To the point where it was almost rhythmic and being sung. He went back and forth between us like he was playing a musical instrument, but instead of an instrument, he used that damn yellow bat. Each time he hit me I swore my head was going to fall off, but luckily it didn't. That day I stopped counting the knots on my head. I was just thankful Father heard farmer Larry's tractor coming back up the road.

That day he stood there beside us as Larry was passing through saying, "I'm just teaching these girls how to swing a bat, Larry. Man, they just swing like a bunch of girls." He said with a chuckle. Lynn and I looked at each other fighting back the tears and waving at Larry knowing that if we started crying we would get beat again.

To this day I can't stand the look of a yellow whiffle ball bat. I swear I could still hear the faint echoing sound as it hit our heads that day every time, I saw one.

Chapter Ten

Just Trying to Stay Alive

THAT WINTER WE HAD SEVERAL BLIZZARDS causing early dismissals and school to be canceled. It almost became like Groundhog Day, waking up each morning being told there was no school and to go back to bed. We missed so many days that winter in the state of Ohio waived snow days because there were so many. Otherwise, we would have been making days up most of the summer.

Where most children cheered for being at home with their parents there was no celebration at our house. Those amazing, magical days were for others so they could sleep in as late as they wanted, and play outside in the snow making snow angels, snowmen, and igloos. By then we were simply trying to stay ahead of the abuse and psychological mind games but failing miserably at it. Most children spent their childhood reflecting on snow days like it was a magical event, holding onto memories of the excitement of watching the television screen call for a snowbird day. I sat in anticipation for a whole other reason. Biting my nails I read one by one as the schools near and far called for cancellations or a delay, then it happened Harrison Hills City School District. I sat there and immediately started panicking, reflecting on all of the what-ifs and I hope not. As I was shutting the television off, I noticed just how cold it felt to have gotten since being up and getting ready for school. I recall trying to dry my hair before school, trying not to make a sound for fear that it would wake father up. It was a trick that Kay taught me many years prior.

By this time in mother and father's marriage, he seemed to take a liking to sleeping on the couch where mother slept in the bedroom, so we had to be extra quiet when we got ready for school. I remember one time while Kay was trying to get ready for school her curling iron fell onto the floor waking her father up. She got her ass handed to her that morning before school when her father beat her with the yellow wiffle ball bat. You could hear her screaming, and yelling. The echoes of her cries could be heard throughout the trailer.

Another time Kay was lying on the heater trying to dry her hair because we couldn't use the dryer for fear it would wake her father and mother. Many mornings, we lay overtop the heater attempting to dry our hair.

I went to the linen closet and pulled another blanket down because it was extremely cold. Then, I tried doing what we called "bumping the heat" meaning you kept it on the same digit but you bumped it so the heat would kick on.

I did this several times until finally, Father woke up. "What the fuck did you do now? Let me guess you're bumping the heat to dry your hair?" Father said. "No, father my hair is already dry, but school was canceled. I noticed I started to see my breath while I was watching for cancellations. I decided to bump the heat to attempt for it to come on. "Mother fucker, you've got to be kicking me." father shouted. By this time, he was already over to the thermostat. Why in the fuck isn't this coming on?" He said as he was fidgeting with the thermostat. By now he had the heater door open looking at it.

It would start then shut down, start then shut down. Father was having problems figuring out what was wrong with a piece of shit as he would say. I stood there like a brainwashed soldier, not being able to move, having an inkling of what would come next. He stood up quickly, his pj's almost falling. As he turned around, he slapped me a crossed the face, yelling "What the fuck did you do?" "Nothing, I did nothing," I spoke quietly making sure not to wake Mother. "Yeah, I just fucking bet," Father said. I stood there not moving, just staring at him. The air could be cut with a knife between us two.

Something was different that day, I'm not sure if he finally saw someone who wasn't going to put up with his shit or was surprised at how well I took his slap a crossed my face. Either way, the mood was intense. It wasn't until years later that my father realized just how done I was with his and my mother's bullshit.

We also fed the outside animals right after school, but since there was none that day, we fed them a little bit early due to the plummeting wind chills we were expecting that night. We would mix what little bit of scraps into the dog food during the winter months in an attempt to keep them somewhat heavier.

Mother stood in the kitchen mixing creamed peas and some other expired food into the bucket along with regular hard dog food. "Lynn, get the dog's food and take it out to them. Make it fast. It's cold out there." Mother yelled.

"I'll go outside with her mother." I stated, "No, it's too cold out and that's not good for your asthma." Mother said. I just stood there and nodded, but thought, What about Lynn and her heart condition? I often wondered if they ever cared and considered that.

Lynn came out bundled up with a few layers of jeans and tops on because of having to walk through the 18-plus inches of snow we got the night before. The snow hit her just above the knee, making it difficult to walk in.

Lynn took the food out and a warm bucket of water in hopes it would help break up the ice on the bucket of water that was already there at Crystal's doghouse.

Some time passed by, and Mother asked if Lynn had come back in, by now it was getting darker outside. "No, Mother she hasn't. I can go check on her." I spoke. "Well, okay, but make it fast with your asthma, and as cold as it is outside, you'll have an attack, and we don't need that," she said. I bundled up nice and warm making my way outside.

The snow had started back up again along with the wind. It was blistering cold out, which pierced through my body causing me to take a deep a breath then an almost shaking movement to "shake the cold off."

I looked up at the Crystal's doghouse, but Lynn wasn't there, I looked up at the playhouse where the chickens and turkey once lived, she wasn't there either. Where on earth could she be? I mumbled to myself. In fact, after taking a better look around, there were no footprints on Crystals box or the old playhouse.

With the time lapse and blowing snow it was hard to make out what was a footprint and snowdrift. As I made my way to the end of the run-down trailer, I spotted something in the snow, it was Lynn's footprints which lead to the shed by the driveway. As I was walking over there pushing my way through the snow, I thought, "Oh, my God, this will be it. This will be how Lynn's found dead from her heart giving out.

I reached the shed, but Lynn wasn't outside. I slowly opened it. There Lynn was hunched over, eating the dog food that mother had mixed up with scraps. "Lynn, what on earth are you doing?" I said in a high-pitched excited voice.

Lynn jumped and stared at me like a deer in headlights. "Lynn, I said in a whispering voice, "What are you doing? Why are you eating dog food?" Big crocodile tears swelled up, as she stood there with a scoop of dog food in her hand. "Trisha, I'm hungry I'm just so hungry," Lynn exclaimed. I couldn't help but almost feel sick to my stomach as I watched the creamed peas drip back down into the dog food bucket.

"Lynn, it's okay. Put that back down. I'll help you hurry up and feed Crystal, so you don't get into trouble. Lynn stood there staring at me, "Please, don't tell mother or father. I don't want to get beat again." Lynn said.

As I looked at her oval skin, I noticed that she didn't have the beautiful complexion that she once had, it was paler." "It's okay Lynn your secret is safe with me," I said as I was hugging her. It was then that I noticed how thin she was. I could feel her spine and ribs. She was doing so well with her weight gain while at the detention center, and now this. I caught myself hugging her just a little tighter that day. "Ok wipe your tears away let's hurry because mother is coming looking for us," I spoke in a humbling manner.

She wiped her eyes and placed her hand into the snow making sure that the scraps from several nights' prior were all wiped clean. "Now, hurry up before we get into trouble, Lynn. Hurry up walk faster." I yelled.

By this time, my feet felt so cold, almost numb. Finally, we reached Crystal's box where she was tucked all snug into the corner trying to stay warm. I reached in, "It's okay girl. I wish I could take you inside with us where it's warmer. I'm sorry girl. I'm so sorry." I whispered as I was petting her matted coat.

"Hurry up Trisha lets go." When we got back to the trailer, mother asked, "What the fuck took so long?" "Oh, sorry Mother the snow was so thick it was hard for Lynn to walk through, so I helped her," I said with a smile.

Lynn still taking her clothes off at the door looked up with the saddest face and mouthed, "Thank you." I winked at her without Mother noticing, being that she had her head downplaying her handheld game of Yahtzee.

It was that night that I realized just how deprived Lynn was of food. To eat scraps and dog food just to try to stay alive is called desperate times. The thought of it made my eyes swollen with tears. To think of a person doing that just to survive and to feel so dehumanized was uncalled for. No human being should've ever gone through what she of all people went through.

Chapter Eleven

Pantry Closet

LYNN BY THIS TIME HAD BEEN in and out of Fox Run and Job and Family Services was in and out of the house. No day went by that we didn't fear for what was about to come.

Each time Job and Family Services came Mother gave them the same song and danced. How couldn't her father possibly do such things as Lynn was suggesting at the Fox Run? One time Job and Family Services showed up. Mother almost looked frozen. Like, for the first time she knew, they were catching her in lies. She stood there like a deer in the headlights.

When mother opened the door, the lady said she was Beckie from Job and Family Services. She was a very tall, broad shoulder, heavy set, and would even say an Amazon woman. She had dark, short curly hair, a mullet like the eighty's women would sport. Her jeans barely covered her long legs, and her plaid shirt made her look like a farmer. Her voice was masculine, and she had a dry smoker's cough.

Mother invited her in, and they had a seat at the kitchen table. "What brings you here Beckie," Mother asked in a casual voice. "Well, there seems to have been another complaint, Candy. The complaint said that Lynn was in this food pantry hiding trying to get away from you, while you were kicking her, all while she was in the closet." Beckie stated. "Now, Beckie, how on earth could I kick her while she was in the pantry?" Mother said. "Is Lynn home?" Beckie said. "LYNN! Looks like you've got company. Do you mind coming out here?" Mother yelled.

Lynn came around the corner with her head down. She always seemed defeated anymore. So sad and one of the worst self-esteems one could have. Do you blame her though? Although daily beatings, especially from their mother, she was the worst of the two. He seemed to have laid off the abuse with Lynn being mother did enough for both.

"Yes, mother," Lynn whispered. "This is Beckie. She's here from Job and Family Services. She claims that someone turned me in for abusing you again." Mother started with a warning tone of voice. That voice was a voice we all heard from time to time.

"Hello, Beckie," Lynn whispered. Her head was still down, staring at her feet the whole. Her black hair lay on her face and from time-to-time Lynn would push it back. Her oversized sweatshirt made her look almost twice as big, not that twice as big would be bad considering how small Lynn was.

'Lynn there was a report that you were being kicked by your mother in the pantry. Is that true?" Beckie asked. For the first time, Lynn looked up, not even looking towards Mother. "Yes," Lynn whispered. "Ok, Lynn please show me. How she was kicking you inside the pantry." "Candy, I want you to show me how you could kick Lynn while in the pantry," Beckie stated.

Lynn climbed to the corner of the pantry moving the dog food out of the way which wasn't there a few days prior and placed it back in front of her. That was Lynn's mistake not thinking about the dog food, not being there on the day that their mother was kicking Lynn for not doing her chores.

Mother stood there in front of the pantry trying to kick Lynn, but the dog food bag was in front of Lynn. The look of defeat was on Lynn's face once again for not being able to prove that Mother was kicking her. As much as Mother tried her legs couldn't reach with the dog food in the way.

That day even if Lynn had proven what Mother had done, I'm sure Beckie would have still turned the cheek. You see Beckie was related on their father's side, a second cousin to him. So, she turned a blind eye and went on about her day.

"Candy, I'm so sorry to have bothered you. It looks like Lynn's been lying once again. I'll put this on record that I was here, and until Lynn calls or other reports are made you won't see me again." Beckie said. "I would say it was nice seeing you Beckie, but these circumstances are never nice." Mother replied. "You should consider sending her back to Fun Fox being she still hasn't learned her lesson from all the lies she likes to tell, Candy," Beckie said in a pissed-off tone. "You know Lynn, this is ridiculous, wasting my time to come out here only to see more lies being told. You've got a good mother and father. When your biological mother left you with your father signing her rights over, that proved she wanted nothing to do with you. Here you have Candy who stepped up to be the mother you didn't have when your father met her. Yet you want to continue to spread lies. Why, is that Lynn?" Beckie said in an angry tone of voice. Lynn went to say something back, but Beckie put her hand up as if to say stop, she didn't want to hear it.

Surprisingly, mother and father didn't do anything to Lynn that evening when father returned home. I overheard mother say something about, "Lynn, was embarrassed and that was enough for her for the day. Knowing that nobody believes the bitch was enough for her.

If only Job and Family Services had known that Beckie was related maybe things would have been different that visit. Maybe someone at the office would have sent someone else to investigate. Or perhaps they already knew but didn't care.

Chapter Twelve

The Apple Doesn't Fall Too Far from the Tree

OUR LIVES ABSOLUTELY AND UTTERLY SUCKED but for one of us it was a bit worse. Lynn without a doubt had the worst of it all at least in my opinion. However, I also gave Lynn my fair share of undeniable pain and suffering which I am not proud of. In fact, although I have forgiven myself over the years because I was just a little girl who had her own fair share of ass beatings and abuse. I started mimicking my mother's abusive ways towards Lynn. I know today as an adult that children at a young age are literally being groomed by their parents from day one. For the longest time I hated what I had done to Lynn. My hate grew so much towards myself that I even attempted suicide when I was around 13 years old by taking a bunch of pills. That day I'm not quite sure why God didn't take me home, other than it wasn't my time to go. It was a cold November day; your breath could be seen from the chilly temperatures. Mother as a form of punishment would spray Lynn off with the garden hoses, temperatures permitting so that the hose wouldn't freeze. I swear mother was just as bad as the mental hospitals back in the day that practiced hydrotherapy as a form of punishment.

Back in the 20th century hydrotherapy was used for a variety of different situations including suicide tendencies, aggressive behavior, and manic depression. Doctors in the day believed by inducing fear by using hoses like the firefighters use to spray their patience's that it will help disordered their brain back to being normal. However, this was abuse back then and it's abuse now. There was nothing normal about this. It took a very sick, twisted, narcistic person, and downright evil to do what she especially did to Lynn. It was one of mother's ways of disciplining Lynn when she acted up, but now as I'm older and reflecting, Lynn really wasn't the problem, neither was Kay, nor myself. We were molded to do the unthinkable to Lynn or we'd get beat within an inch of our lives. Lynn stood there in just her bra and underwear trying to cover up her private areas as mother used was spraying her off. "Turn baby Lynn, now let me get your back." Mother yelled. Mind you, this is the middle of November when the temperatures are typically in the low 50's with an ice-cold hose being used on a 16-year-old that has a heart condition. Lynn stood there crying, shaking, and yelling how cold she was but mother didn't care, nor did she stop. The longer Lynn cried the more mother stood there spraying her. "Have you had enough bitch?" Mother yelled. "Yes, mother I've had enough. I promise I won't forget to feed the dogs again. I'll do better mother!" Lynn pleaded. Lynn stood there more defeated than I've ever seen. She was a walking, living, breathing skeleton, due to not being fed properly. Her coloration was being coming greyish, her lips even more blue and purple. She stood there shaking violently as if she was having a seizure, but she wasn't she was just that cold. You could hear her teeth chattering against each other uncontrollably. Her long black hair was something that Lynn always admired, it was absolutely gorgeous, but it was laying a crossed her back and face making her look like some sort of monster from a horror movie. I question if at one point she wasn't experiencing hypothermia.

We'll never know though, because being taken to the hospital was off limits for the obvious reason, unless of course it involved Fox Run. "You better not forget to feed the dogs again or what you'll get next will be much worse than this you little cunt!" Mother screamed as she was shutting the hose off. "Yes, mother." Lynn said in between her teeth chattering. "Oh, one more thing, go get me the scissors and a chair, I'm going to trim your hair." Mother said as she firmly pressed her lips to her mouth. "Yes, mother." Lynn said. "Get dressed. I wouldn't want you to freeze to death. How would I ever explain that one?" Mother said as she gloated and chuckled with an evil laugh following. I followed Lynn to the trailer, I could see her spine showing, each vertebra protruding from her emaciated frame, along with her ribs, and bruises still there from her beating beat before. Her long black hair hit midways down her back and it was the one thing that she had confidence with. "Lynn, are you okay?" I asked in between tears. "I'll be fine. Don't I always make it through this shit?" Lynn snapped.

It was unlike Lynn to have a ton with me, but after what she went through, I didn't blame her. Lynn quickly got dressed throwing on jeans, a dark sweater, some socks but the only thing she could find was the ones with holes in them, and her ratty-looking bra. Underwear and bras were never on the top priority list to buy so we made do with what we had, even having to share the same underwear. It wasn't ideal but what else was we supposed to do? Lynn grabbed the chair, scissors, taking them to the front porch wear mother was waiting. She stood there with a look of shear evil, like the type of evil you see when people in movies get possessed by a demon on the horror movies. She was evil and mean but this day was the day that put the icing on the cake for Lynn. Lynn handed mother the scissors and placed the chair onto the porch making sure not to put the legs into the holes. "This won't take but a minute Lynn, I'm just going to give you a nice old trim." Mother said with authority. Lynn sat down; she was still shaking almost uncontrollably from being so cold. I sat there watching as mother was cutting Lynn's dead ends off.

Each time mother would come close to Lynn she would flinch. We were so used to just getting back handed, beat with the whiffle ball bat, or that damn rolled newspaper wrapped in black tape that it was common to see us girls flinch but it was Lynn that did it the most. Lynn's hair was in fact needing trimmed, but what was about to happen would change not only her but me forever. Lynn's hair was falling onto the porch, covering it the wood around her, landing on her and causing her to start to scratch from her hair landing on her. Mother grabbed her by the back of her head making sure to wrap her hands tightly around Lynn's hair and jerked it saying, "Hold the fuck still, Lynn!" "OUCH." Lynn screeched and began to cry. Mother stopped what she was doing and stood in front of Lynn, "Are you crying? What the fuck are you crying for? I'll give you something to cry about bitch!" Mother said as she was talking through her teeth. It was then that mother grabbed Lynn's hair making a high ponytail affect and before a reaction could even be done. Mother chopped Lynn's hair off. It was so short and uneven at this point that it looked like a boy's haircut. "NOOOOOOOO, why would you do that? I can't believe you just cut my fucking hair like that." Lynn said in a raging voice. Lynn jumped up in a hostile manner, tears streaming down her face.

Mother was standing in front of Lynn at the corner of the porch the highest part and that's when it happened. "Fucking cunt, ass baby. Your fucking hair will grow back. You shouldn't have pissed me off." Mother stood there screaming. I was standing on the sidewalk shaking, because any time there was yelling it would make me scared. "My hair was the only thing pretty about me! My hair is now gone because of you. I hate you! I hate you!" Lynn screamed at the top of her lungs. You could hear her screams echoing a crossed the countryside that day. It wasn't the typical screams of pain and torture from being abused. It was that of hate, anger, and rage. It was a rage I've never seen from Lynn, but that of our own father. "Shut the f...." mother went to say, but before she completed the sentence.

Lynn shoved her backwards; mother stumbled over the chair and fell onto the ground. There she laid motionless, I thought for a second that she was dead. I felt something that day that I never felt before, my body began to shake, but not from fear it was from absolute rage. It was overwhelming, intense, I could feel a sense of energy running through my body that was uncontrollable. My hands and forehead began to sweat, my rate was racing so much I thought it was going to come out of my chest. Lub-DUM, Lub-DUM, Lub-DUM, I could hear my heart echoing. It was then something else happened I started to see everything around me go black and the only thing I could focus in on was Lynn as she was standing on the porch peering over the edge with gratitude for what she did.

Then I charged Lynn, I screaming, "What the fuck Lynn, you killed mother. You fucking killed mother. You fucking dumb ass fucking bitch!! Who the fuck do you think you are? Huh? In that moment of time that I swear my feet didn't hit those steps that I was standing in front of Lynn. Although I was half her height my weight suppressed Lynn's by at least 20 pounds. Before Lynn could speak, before she could explain her actions, or her reasoning behind what she did. Even though now as an adult I don't blame her for what she did, in fact I'm actually proud of her for finally taking the stand and dishing out what mother was doing to her all along.

I was so young at only 10 years old I didn't look at it that way. It was then, I grabbed Lynn's hair that remained and threw her to the ground. I sat on her and threw punches like I was a man that day, not of a 10-year-old. Punch after punch, all Lynn was capable of doing was trying to protect her face as I sat on top of her swinging left and right. At one point I even grabbed ahold of her head and started hitting it off the porch. Lynn grabbed her head with both hands and let out a screamed, of anguish. It was then I heard mother, scream, "Trisha, stop before you kill her. Get the fuck off of her." It was the voice of mother. Hearing her voice did no good, I was in full blackout mode. All I could hear was the faint whimpers of Lynn and screams from mother. It was then that I heard, "KID GET THE FUCK UP RIGHT NOW!" It was father standing behind me. "Candy, don't just stand there do something!" Father screamed. They tried to pull me off her but it was no good, my legs were wrapped around Lynn's. I barely remember hearing the door open and just like many times before, "BOOM, BOOM, BOOM!" It was father shooting the gun overtop our heads. It was then and only then that I stopped. I jumped up with an adrenaline high and shoved father backwards into the door. It was then he grabbed me by my head and smashed my face off of the door frame, blood began to pour from my face. "Now, stop it kid!" Father screamed.

I was stunned at what just happened, then it was followed by immediate remorse for what I did to poor Lynn. There she laid on the porch with her hands covering her face, surrounded by her hair that mother just butchered, bleeding from her mouth. Lynn pitiful sobs were gut wrenching. I dropped beside her, "Lynn, I'm sorry. I'm so sorry Lynn. I don't understand what just happened. Please forgive me." I sat on my knees next to her begging for forgiveness. However, I wouldn't get the reassurance that it would be okay from her. She just laid there, screaming, shaking, and making horrible noises from being in pain. "What the fuck did I just walk into Candy? Why is Lynn's hair all over the porch? Why were the kids fighting and why do you have grass stain all over your back and front of your shirt?" Father screamed without giving much time for her to answer in between. She never did answer why Lynn's hair was on the porch, common sense would have told someone that Lynn just got her hair cut.

However, she told father that Lynn jumped while she was cutting her hair causing mothers scissors to slip taking off all of her hair. Then, Lynn got pissed off and pushed me off the porch and Trisha beat Lynn's ass for doing so. Father had heard enough and grabbed me by the top part of my hair and pulled me into the house where he made me strip down, spread my legs, and put my hands flat against the wall. He then got the rolled-up newspaper covered in black tape and began to swing hitting me from the top of my head to the bottoms of my feet. Feet was a thing with father too, he'd make up pick our feet up and smack them with his choice of object. I lost count at how many times he hit me, all I know is I started focusing on everything but what he was doing so I would move and get hit more. I stood there like the solider he was making me out to be. That day changed not only me, but Lynn forever. It was the day we both lost our shit finally. It was the day that all of our built-up anger from the way mother and father abusing us came out in the most rageful way yet, or was it?

Chapter Thirteen

The Final Straw

IT WAS MIDWAY THROUGH LYNN'S JUNIOR year when life as it has always been with our dysfunctional family would change for the rest of our lives. Nothing ever changed, for the better it was about to get much worse.

Mother had woken Lynn and me up for school. "Girls, get the fuck up I slept through the alarm you do not have much time to get ready. The bus will be here in about 20 minutes. That morning, I was moving extra slowly and decided to go to school in the plaid pajamas and sweatshirt I wore to bed. I was exhausted. Father would still creep into our bedroom and playhouse occasionally, now that he was sleeping on the couch more often, he made sure he would come in to pay a visit. Sometimes it would be just me, other times it would involve Lynn. I always hated those nights, but what were we supposed to do? He would kill us if we said a word.

I remember hearing chaos coming from the living room. Mother was sitting on the couch under the brown and cream-colored Afghan blanket. I heard Mother screaming, "Okay baby Lynn since I cannot trust you. Take your shoes off and empty them." I am not sure what there was nothing to trust but come on she did not do anything. She did not go anywhere. She only had one friend who was not allowed to come to the house, because his mother had connections to Job and Family Services. So, God forbid someone might catch on to what was happening at that dump we called home. Besides, even if he did Shawn was just like Lynn, they were in the special educational classes at school and although it was not mentally retarded they were both borderline. I do not think between the two of them they'd even know how to make a proper report because their reading and writing skills were lacking. Lynn complied emptying her shoes one by one showing that there was nothing inside. "Socks, now Lynn!" Mother said demanding! Just like before with Lynn's shoes she took her socks out and turned

them inside out showing there was nothing hidden inside. Lynn
bent over and went to put her socks back on and shoes, but her
mother was not having them. "What do you think you are
doing? I say who. I say how. I say when. "Yes, mother," Lynn
said with a cracking voice. "Now take your pants off and repeat
the process, but first empty your pants pockets. Lynn repeated
and there was nothing. "Throw your pants on the couch! Hurry
up, Lynn. Now, take your underwear off. I cannot be too sure
with you anymore." Mother said in an annoyed voice. "My
underwear, why my underwear?" Lynn said in a whisper from
being embarrassed. "What part of taking them off now do not
you get Lynn? Do you want me to get the yellow bat? Do you?"
Mother screamed. Before she could even finish her sentence
there Lynn stood without any shoes, no socks, no pants, and
now no underwear. She stood there embarrassed and ashamed
as anyone would be trying to cover up. "Bend over Lynn and
spread your ass cheeks." Mother said with authority. "No, I'm
not doing that!" Lynn screamed with tears filling her brown
eyes. "No, you are not doing that? Do it now. The bus will be
here and if you miss God help you, Lynn. God fucking help
you!" Mother screamed. Lynn stood there hesitantly and finally
bent over and spread her butt cheeks. "Hurry up and get
dressed, Lynn." Mother said with an annoyed voice like she was
hoping for something to fall out of Lynn. What type of sick
fucking person, let alone a mother does that to her child? Lynn
quickly got dressed throwing on her clothes so fast that when
she was putting her shoes on, she fell. "Jesus, fucking Christ
Lynn get up!" Mother stood over her and all Lynn could do was
lay there in anticipation of Mother to start swinging on her. I
ran over and helped Lynn up. "Come on Lynn," I whispered. As
she was taking my hand and getting her footing, she grabbed
her bookbag and went to hold out the door. "One more thing
Lynn." Mother said with pressed lips. "Yes, mother." "Take
your shirt and bra off. Make sure you shake them out. NOW

LYNN!" Mother said in an angry tone of voice. Lynn was fumbling trying to get her shirt unbuttoned. When a white note fell from underneath her shirt. It caught Lynn by surprise as if she had forgotten that it was there. She quickly bent over and went to reach for it. However, Mother stomped on it, covering it with her foot. "Don't please don't." Lynn cried. "Don't what Lynn." Mother said with a shitty smirk. "Read it?" "Yes, please don't," Lynn asked in a pleading voice. "Oh, look it's a note and Mother began to read it."

Deer Shawn,

I just wunted to say I luv u!

Luv Lynn

Mother then busted up laughing with tears rolling down her eyes with excitement from embarrassing Lynn from reading her first love letter. Lynn stopped getting underdressed and just stood there, with a blank look on her face. "Can I have that back please?" Lynn whimpered. Mother threw the letter into her face, still making fun of Lynn for her spelling mistakes. It was then that the bus pulled up and saved Lynn that day.

We took off like a bad out of hell, running to the bus being sure not to miss it, and having a seat together. Lynn was upset and crying, and I reached over, grabbing her hand as she flinched, thinking that I was about to smack her, which at this point I did often to get her attention. "Lynn, stop your fucking crying. You wouldn't want mother and father to get a call from the school would you, saying you're upset?" I asked in a whispering voice. Lynn wiped her tears away and straightened up her shirt which was still partly unbuttoned. "Trisha, promise me something, please. Take care of yourself and don't allow them to continue the abuse with you." Lynn said this in a manner as if she was leaving and never coming back. I was only eleven at the time and didn't catch onto where she was going with her comments. "I promise Lynn," I whispered. The bus ride was quiet between us two, with the occasional Lynn saying, "You'll be just fine."

When Lynn got off the bus she looked back over her shoulder as if she were saying goodbye one last time mouthing the words, "I love you." I waved at her, sticking my tongue out, and mouthed "I love you." back to Lynn. Little did I know just how important those words would be.

The day was short, only half a day due to parent-teacher conferences that afternoon, Mother had stopped at the school to pick Lynn and me up. I saw her old Cutlas from afar and walked my way over pulling my bookbag down to the side. I hopped in the front seat and investigated the back, but Lynn wasn't there. "Hello Mother, how was your day?" I asked with a smile. She looked over puzzled as if to say, "Why are you in a good mood?" "I'm doing okay Trisha. How was your day?" Mother asked, which was even stranger because she never cared to ask how my day was ever.

It was time for Lynn's bus to pull up being that her bus was coming from Scio. We watched as the buses pulled in one by one letting the junior high and high school walkers off, but Lynn didn't get off our bus. Mother looked at me almost scared and asked, "Had I seen her." "No, Mother I haven't seen Lynn except for this morning when we got off the bus so she could catch the high school bus," I spoke in a monotone. Mother pulled out of the parking lot and up to our bus, "Hey, Ed that was our bus driver, is Lynn on the bus?" Mother said with a crackling in her voice as if she knew she was in deep shit. Ed looked at the back of the bus. "No, she's not on Candy," Ed said. Mother began to panic, crying nonstop, and hitting the steering wheel as she sped off, circling the school a few times making sure that she simply didn't miss her. Lynn was nowhere to be found. Lynn was gone, but where could she be?

When Mother got home, she called the family and asked them if they had seen or heard from Lynn. You know Mother though, she didn't know why Lynn was gone, or what made her upset this time. Things were never the mother or father's fault according to her. Everything was always Lynn's fault. Nobody saw Lynn or heard from her that she called. Lynn was simply gone, vanished.

It wasn't until later that night that the sheriff's cars pulled into the driveway. Their red, white, and blue lights flashed all over the yard as they were talking to their mother and father. There is the sheriff himself standing, "Good evening, Candy and Randy." The sheriff spoke with a deeper tone of voice and that of someone who smoked a lot. "Did you find her?" Mother yelled in an excited voice. "Why, yes we did," he said. "Where is she? When can we pick her up?" Mother asked with tears in her eyes. Father stood there anxiously to hear. "Well, you're not! There seems to be a problem that was brought to our attention about you stripe searching her this morning before school." The sheriff said as if he was rolling his eyes. "Now, for the safety and well-being of Lynn, she's going to be staying with your brother Randy from now on." He said with a stern tone. "All right, why's that?" Father asked in a dumbfounded voice. "Well, since we've been friends for so long, I'm willing to sweep this under the rug because otherwise Job and Family Services will step in and take both girls. Now, you don't want that now do you?" he asked. "Wait you mean to tell me she's not coming home sheriff?" Mother and father said at the same time. "That's exactly what I mean if you don't want your good reputation with the community ruined and Trisha not to be pulled from the house. We'll pretend this never happened because Lynn is of age." He spoke. "WELL, I guess if that's the only choice!" Mother snapped. The sheriff got into his car and pulled out, but mother and father just stood there, not moving.

Finally, the door slammed open "It's all your fault you little bitch that Lynn left and isn't allowed to come back." Mother screamed. I was confused, to say the least. "What do you mean Lynn's not coming back?" I asked. She's gone, she moved in with Uncle Gerald." Mother said. Father looked at me and backhanded me. "What did you do kid?" Father screamed. "I didn't do anything," I said. "That's not true, Trisha told me that Lynn shoved something under her clothes this morning and I had to strip search her." Mother screamed. Father went to get the whiffle bat and began to swing like he'd never swung before, hitting my head, face, shoulders, back, legs, and bottom of my feet. I couldn't stand, I couldn't sit. I just took it thinking to myself what a lying bitch mother was and that's not what had happened that morning. It was then I said to myself that Lynn was gone that I burst into tears. No wonder she said what she said today I thought. She knew she wasn't coming back. I wasn't crying because of being hit. I was crying because I was left all alone with these monsters that claimed to be parents.

It wasn't until years later that I would learn about the sheriff's connection to the first women serial killer and how his own life could have spiraled out of control if things hadn't been different. He would have been concerned about the three little girls who were being beaten, starved, raped, and sodomized by their flesh.

Chapter Fourteen

Tables About to Turn

LYNN IS GONE NOW JUST OVER 2 YEARS. The last time I saw her was that day she had got off the bus. Besides, after Lynn ran away from home that last time I was warned by my mother and father exactly what would happen to me if I contacted her, so I simply didn't. I knew she had moved in with my Uncle Gerald, but we were not close at all. He was my father's brother. I wasn't close to my father's side at all. My mother always said they hated having the Howards bloodline in me which was my mother's birth name. My mother's side didn't like me at all that much either, due to having the McGee bloodline. You see when mother and father got married it was controversial around the community almost causing outrage amongst them. They were shocked because the mother's side of the family had money and came from an exceptional group of people or so they claimed, all because they had nice jobs, and homes, and made a decent living. On the McGee side, most didn't work, lived off the welfare system, had too many kids to keep track of, and didn't have the best reputation due to drugs and alcohol usage. It wasn't until later in life that we were told that the only reason mother married father was due to money that she thought he had because during the time they met he was a coal miner. It wasn't long after they married that he lost his job from falling down a coal mining shaft. After that he never held down another job, it was odd jobs just trying to make it by. So, if Mother thought she was marrying into money she was by far mistaken, and Father had the last laugh.

As for me, it was so hard trying to have a normal life with both sides of my family, not liking me due to the bloodlines, and the older I got the more lies my mother would tell the family about me. I was only thirteen when my mother started telling the family the unthinkable that I was on drugs and drinking. The fact of the matter was that I didn't do any of that until her lies started to consume me from the inside out.

My Gram couldn't even look at me anymore and Pap well he had passed away so that was at least one less person who didn't look at me with disappointment. My Aunt Tillie, who I swear hated me from birth started bullying me by now more than not, her constant jabs and digs got to me in an almost indescribable way. Between her twisted facial expressions, or simply asking me what types of drugs I was on, or my all-time favorite statement, "You give your mother too much grief. That's my sister you should help more around the house and stop being so lazy!" Aunt Tillie would exclaim. I was too young, and she was one of the people who used to scare me the most. I'm not sure why I never stuck up for myself, other than the sheer terror that I felt every time I was around her. Mother molded our family by the time we reached adulthood to downright hate, disown, and snub us acting like we were nonexistent. Without them saying we were dead to them; we might have well been. All this because mother was a pathological liar, who could not stand for someone else to get attention. giving me shit so why not just start doing what Mother was lying about? I was only thirteen but so sick and tired of life that I couldn't stand looking at myself in the mirror any longer.

It was one day after softball practice that I caved to peer pressure and smoked my first joint. I hated the way it made me feel, but I hated the way that I felt before I took my first hit. I typically would walk to and from softball practice like Kay did all those years, but on this day, I decided to stay at the park and walk towards a group of kids that I knew from school There they stood huddled in the corner of the white building that served sandwiches, hotdogs, refreshments, and chips. Their way of attempting not to be seen as unsuccessful by far, being stuck out like sore thumbs with their black outfits, rocker hair, and obnoxiously loud voices. "Hey, Trisha, what is up? Get over here come talk to us!" One teen said as if they were leaning up against the building. As I looked around, I saw some of them smoking those nasty cigarettes that Mother smoked. Their deep laughter filled the air as they were joking about getting caught "smoking." I had no clue what they were passing around that day until finally, they asked me to take a hit. "No, I'm good," I said as I went to walk away. "Pussy, you are fucking pussy as bitch." One boy said who looked the most ridiculous with his chains wrapped around his waist, wrist, and hanging from his hip. He was wearing black over pants attempting to look like an inner gangster in our country setting. Then, it hit me, these kids were making fun of me the way most have my whole young life. I did not want that to happen, so I turned around and said, "You know what, yeah I'll take a hit or whatever the fuck you call it." All were taken by surprise and laughed when they heard me talking like that because up until this point, never cussed around them, at school, or in front of my parents. "Here, take a hit," Larry said with a smirk. He had the most beautiful blue eyes besides his mother's and a contagious smile. I don't believe he ever really knew just how handsome he was. It was then I took it from his hands, placing my lips around it. "Nigger lips! Good God, do not smoke it like that!" One scream startled me being I was still being screamed at home. He showed me how to pinch it off and there it happened I took my first hit of pot, dope, reefer, Mary Jane, or whatever you want to call it. The smell was awful unless you like the smell and taste of skunky letting its ass off in your mouth. If that is a smell you prefer, then the smell is refreshing. I started to feel dizzy, everything began to spin, and I was becoming relaxed, euphoric if you will. I did not understand what was happening. I never felt like this before, all I knew was it felt amazing. The kids were laughing saying I was tripping and how spaced out I was. Which caused me to start laughing. We all stood there laughing like a clan of hyenas and finally, everything began to spin. I did not want to say anything, so I just walked off.

It was a longer walk home than normal because I was so tired from practice and now my first usage of reefer. Everything felt like it was dragging, my feet did not want to walk or so it felt. I swear that walk home that day was the longest in history for me. I finally reached the house, thankfully nobody was there. Mother was taking nursing classes in Steubenville and God only knows where Father was and honestly, I could give to fucks less providing he was not there to playhouse with me. I walked into the house and although we only had one cat, the smell of cat piss hit me in the face. I grabbed water and leftover pizza from a few days prior and laid in my room eating it like I had not eaten in weeks. I could not understand what this feeling was, but it caused me to eat half a box of pizza. It would be later I'd find out what I was experiencing was the commonly known case of the munches.

The next morning was Saturday which meant Mother was making me go to my cousin's wedding reception. He was married in another state and the family who were local were going to celebrate. I am not sure how much pot lasts in someone's system, but that morning I woke up tired, and in a hung-over-like state. I was only thirteen, so that is what I imagined it was. Either way that morning it gave me balls of steel. Mother and father were fighting once again because he did not want her to attend the reception. Fighting was echoing once again throughout that shit-hole trailer. That was my normal way of living and life in my 13 years. I was sitting in the living room trying to eat cereal I should've known better; it was the last of Rice Crispies father's favorite. As he was yelling at his mother in the bedroom, I heard him say, "Just go bitch. Go be with your family. I'm sure they'll be men there you can hang over!" The door slammed behind him as he was walking through the hallway, I heard a loud crash, "God, fucking dammit!" Father screamed. There he was lying on the floor because his foot fell through the rotting hallway floor. He was lying there trying to wiggle his leg out and finally pulled it to safety. I couldn't help but think that day too bad that he didn't get seriously injured. It was then he caught me staring at him, dazed as can be. "What the fuck are you looking at bitch?" He screamed. "Without missing a beat I said, "You know some dumb fuck that caused a hole in the hallway floor from not watching where he was stepping!" That as you can only imagine enraged him. He by now was in my face his nose touching mine like he's done several times before. I just stared at him, not flinching, not moving except to continue to eat my cereal. He slapped me so hard that cereal went flying out of my mouth. Mother screamed, "What the fuck was that for?" "What you didn't hear what the little bitch said?" He then repeated what I said to her. It made her chuckle. "Well, she is your kid after all." She spoke. He went from enraged to irate in seconds. "You are fucking cunt you're just like your daughter! I didn't want her in the first place you insisted on more kids after the boys died! You just stay right there I have something for you bitch!" He screamed. He ran through the hallway almost stepping into the hole he just created. He grabbed Pistol Pete and pointed it right toward me. I jumped up thinking the worst was about to happen. He was continuing to run towards Mother and shoved Pistol Pete under her jaw, "I could kill you right fucking now!" Father screamed while spitting into her face. "Go ahead!" Mother screamed back. Father looked stunned and said, "What did you just say to me?" "Go ahead pull the trigger!" Mother yelled. "That'll be too easy! I'm just going to kill myself. I'll blow my mother fucking brains out in front of you and that bitch right there." He screamed, spitting flying from his mouth like some rabbit dog. "Do it then! What the fuck are you waiting for? Put yourself out of your miserable misery!" Mother screamed once more. I'm not sure if it was the fact that Mother screamed at him in a manner that she never screamed at him before, or he was starting to realize he was slowly starting to lose control of us. However, he let go of Mother and sat on the couch, placing Pistol Pete on the black slate coffee table that sat in the middle of the living room floor. He sat there with a blank face I couldn't tell what he was thinking.

"I'm going to get ready for Dennis's reception." It was Aunt Tillie's son so all I kept thinking of was this would be fun. She already hated me enough. She was like a high school bully to me. I don't know if she ever caught on to the effects of her slide remarks or if it was the fact that she simply didn't care. It was a combination of both, but mostly the fact that she didn't care about the daggers that were coming from her mouth that cut me so deep that I tried killing myself due to her nonsense. Now, I must face her at her son's reception. I fucking hated the fact nobody cared about my feelings or how seeing her was going to affect me. Something was brewing in me, that was explosive. Call it build-up anger, frustration, determination, shit was coming to a head.

I heard mother yelling for me to hurry up and get my ass moving. Do you realize how many times I have heard them make this statement over the last few years? It was then that I truly realized my breaking point finally was coming to a head. Countless times being called a bitch, a cunt, to hurry the fuck up whenever I just started getting ready due to my mother and father only giving me minutes to get ready. There was nothing ordinary about this fucked up family. Between the almost daily beatings at times, to still being forced to playhouse, trying to be a good person even though. The only time I ever felt safe was when I was at my best friend's house, Annie Ryders. What kind of life is this for someone?

The famous phrase came out of my mother's mouth, "I don't have all fucking day! Hurry the fuck up bitch!" Mother screamed. So, I threw my brush down onto the sink and walked into the living room. I wasn't done by far. As I was walking into the living room there my father sat with the gun still on the black slate table, like it was supposed to be taunting us or something. He glanced up at me, "What are you staring at kid?" Father screamed. "When I figure it out, I'll let you know," I replied. "Oh, you think you're really funny now, don't you?" Father asked. "Yes, as a matter of fact, I am pretty fucking funny, but you wouldn't know that now, would you?" I asked in a matter-of-fact tone of voice. "Fuck you. I'm just going to blow my head off and get it over with!" Father said with a crackling voice.

I was not sure if he was about to cry at that moment or not. Regardless, I was sick and tired of the threats. I was over feeling unsafe. I was simply done with all the bullshit. I walked over to the table, picked up Pistol Pete, and put the gun to his head. "Do it. Just simply do it or shut the fuck up about it. I am so sick and tired of all your threats. It is time to make a promise!" I screamed at the top of my lungs at him. I did not care. I did not fuck care at all.

He grabbed the gun from me and screamed, "Do that again and see what fucking happens?" As he put the gun back on the table. I snagged it off the table again and backed up with it. "I could blow your head off and it wouldn't fucking bother me one bit," I screamed. Then took the safety off and dumped the clip out onto the floor. "However, you're such a fucking pussy, who likes to threaten us with an empty gun!" I screamed. I threw the gun onto the dirty floor by now Father wasn't reacting violently he was sitting there in total shock and baffled at what just happened. I was in just as much shock as he was. I yelled at mother and said, "Your bitch is fucking ready. I'm going to the car."

I sat there on the way to the reception in shock still at what had just occurred. I can't believe I grabbed Pistol Pete, threatened to shoot my father, and screamed at him. Up until this point I just took his shit like a good little bitch. Things were certainly about to change, and I was about to give them a run for their money with how out of control I was about to come. They're the ones who created this little bitch and they were about to see what she could do.

Chapter Fifteen

Wedding Bells Are Ringing

The rolling hills of Pennsylvania, also known as Keystone State, have always been one of my favorite states to visit. Crossing over the Fort Pitt Bridge and looking across the water that meets the skyscrapers never gets too old to see. It was always nice seeing the Steelers Stadium, but nothing beat those skyscrapers. When I was a little girl, I would always gaze with excitement every time we'd exit the tunnels. It was like night and day from one side of the tunnels to the other. It was like going through another dimension, a time warp if I must say. At first, the tunnel scared me as a little girl, but the older I got the more breathtaking and amazed I became. The skyscrapers looked like never-ending giants that towered over the people below. The city smell was so much different than the countryside. The city smelt like dirty, used air from a recycle bin, nothing fresh about it. The countryside though was breathtaking, the smell of fresh lilac roamed the hillsides, mixed with a hint of cow manure. Country people were always more friendly than city slickers who were always rushing to make money and did not have enough time to slow down and appreciate life. Although it is a mesmerizing scene because in our area you don't see city life, I wouldn't trade those back country roads for anything.

Kay had moved on after graduating from ICM in Pittsburgh and even fallen in love again with Ryan Grant a young man whom she had met in college. I would like to say that Butchie played a part in bringing them together. I never thought she'd find another love, but by the grace of God, she found love once again.

Planning for the wedding was a whole different task, regardless of how much Kay wanted their mother involved. Like most mothers who wait for years to help plan their daughter's wedding out of excitement, it was quite the opposite. She did not go to watch Kay try on wedding dresses; she didn't go to help pick out the decorations. She was not involved in anything. It is all little girl dreams of the day she would go wedding dress shopping and take their mom's, but Kay would not get to experience that. Mother was completely selfish, throwing a fit, Kay called her later that night wanting to say she found the perfect dress, but Mother was not having it. "Well, that's simply great Kay! How am I going to afford your fucking dress, huh? I am not made from money like your in-laws." Mother ranted and raved. This was Kay's moment, not Mother's. Instead of being excited for her, she was anything but excited. Kay's in-laws did pay for her dress. Judy and Paul were more like her parents than mother and father ever were.

Their wedding was gorgeous in the hills of Pennsylvania. It was a setting from the movies with the mountains in the background you could still see snow caps, the cabin looked like a huge barn with fireplaces, and gorgeous woodwork, which was two stories, and had a lake in the front. It was postcard-worthy. The showstopper inside featured their mint green and white cake was to die for it was several layers and with fountains.

That day was the first day I felt like a princess. I wore a white off-the-shoulder dress that hit my knees, with a darker white floral pattern, mint green shoes, and a mint green cardigan jacket. It was not until years went by; that my dress was mother's way of attempting to ruin Kay's wedding. Who wears a white dress to someone else's wedding?

The wedding itself was beautiful except our mother was insistent on having father walk Kay down the aisle. The look on her face said it all, she did not want this man, who brutally beat, molested, and robbed her of her childhood. If looked could kill father would be dead. Kay could not smile when Ryan and she had their first looks, her facial expression was incredibly angry. After all who could blame her. She stood there with her lips pressed tight with the look of complete and total disgust. So even on Kay's most important day, Mother found diverse ways to ruin her moment. When they asked who gave this woman to be with this man, Father said, "I do." Then leaned in and kissed Kay on the lips instead of the cheek. It was his way of saying, "Kiss your daddy one last time." Kay looked like she wanted to vomit for obvious reasons.

I sat there watching Kay get married to her best friend. I started to feel emotional and wiping tears away. I was so happy for Kay and Ryan. Kay did it, she was moving mountains in so many ways and becoming who she fought all those years to become. I was so overwhelmed with emotions for her. I sat there trying not to have anyone see me cry, but then Aunt Tillie saw me crying. I unfortunately had the pleasure of her sitting next to me. She reached down and shook my leg saying, "Stop that right now." I looked over in shock thinking I was hiding my tears so well, but obviously, that wasn't the case. Aunt Tillie then hit my lap with a tissue, "Wipe your face off now! You are ridiculous. Your sister did not even like you." she whispered.

After the wedding, everyone had their pictures taken and then headed out over to the reception. It was gorgeous already, but after dark the lights were on looked whimsical. I rode with my mother, Gram, and her friend Dawn back to the reception hall. Father was supposed to follow us, but he got lost. Everyone was celebrating with the newlywed couple with music and laughter when I heard the doors slam open. There our father was walking through the small entranceway, "THANKS FOR LEAVING ME FUCKING BREADCRUMBS YOUR SNOBBY ASS FUCKING PITTBURGERS!!" Father screamed like a banshee. It seemed like in the blink of an eye a group of guys and their mother surrounded him. "What seems to be the problem?" One man said. "Randy, what's wrong?" Mother asked. "You know what's fucking wrong I got fucking lost," Father screamed. "Just go leave. Nobody wants you here." Ryan said with a voice of authority. "Why you!" Father said as he went to grab him. Another man stepped in, "That's not necessary." "You're going to leave, or we'll throw you out," Ryan said. "FUCK ALL OF YOUR SNOBBY ASS MOTHER FUCKERS!" Father screamed then slammed the doors back open as he left. The screeching of the tires and gravel being thrown could be heard over the top of the DJ's music.

Poor Kay surrounded by her bridesmaids crying because of the ignorance this stupid fuck just did to her at her wedding. Mother tried to comfort her, but she was not having it and turned away. Mother only did this so she could look like the supportive mother, but she was never like that why try now? Gram always knew just what to say though, "Kay, it will be all right. He is gone. Go enjoy yourself. This is your day, Kay. Do not allow anyone to ruin it. Now get out of here and have fun."

Later, the father-daughter dance did not take place, not that Kay would've wanted that to happen. Instead, Uncle Lawson took his place which worked out great, being that they were close. Kay looked like a princess in her ballroom gown dancing amongst her friends. I have never seen her so happy. She laughed real laughs, instead of fake. She was genuinely happy I believe for the first time.

The following morning as we were helping take Kay's reception decorations down, I could not help but take in the view. The mountains were spectacular, reflecting off the lake below, you could still see your breath being it was mid-April, and the dew was heavy on the blades of grass. Everything was perfect, except one thing, Lynn was not there. The last time I heard from Lynn was that morning she got off the bus. It was like she vanished off the planet. It wouldn't be for a couple more years before we would run into each other by mistake.

As I was loading Gram's car, I made the fatal mistake of locking the keys in the trunk, I tried with everything I had to unlock the trunk before going into the reception hall to meet my fate. Something as simple yet not so simple, got my ass handed to me. I was thinking of a million and one excuses as to why I locked the keys in the trunk and what I could say. I was almost rehearsing what I could say to Mother when I found her. I walked into the reception hall, and she was off in the corner taking down decorations. "Mother, I have something to tell you," I said with my voice cracking for fear of what would come next. She looked up and said that it better be good since I was interrupting her from doing stuff. "Well, I forgot to get the keys out of the trunk, and I locked them inside. I am sorry mother. I tried to get the doors unlocked. I could not." I said crying hysterically by now since I figured she beat my ass within an inch of my life. "What do you mean you locked the keys in the car? Are you that fucking stupid. Why would you put the keys in the trunk, WHY?" Mother screamed and stomped her foot in a high-demand manner. "I am sorry I put them beside my hand so I would not forget them, then I went to close the trunk and before I knew it, I had closed the trunk. I am so sorry. I did not mean to." Stood there shaking as fear went through my body like electricity. It was then she slapped me across the face I felt the instant burning from the red mark that started to form on my cheek. Everyone looked over at the same time because of hearing the loud slap of her hand hitting my face. Her friend Denise chimed in, "What did she do now Candy?" Still, everyone stood there puzzled as to what just transpired. "This brat locked Gram's keys in the car!" Mother exclaimed. "Well, I'm sure she didn't mean to do that Candy." Gram said with a matter-of-fact voice. "What the hell are we going to do?"

Mother screamed. By this time people were making their way out to the car to see if they could get the keys out of the trunk. I was the last one to leave the reception hall.

A couple of Kay's friends tried to get the keys out. It did not do any good. Then, the police officers were called to retrieve the keys from the trunk. This pushed us a couple of hours behind from leaving Pennsylvania before a huge snowfall came.

It was one of the longest drives home because I knew what would happen once, I got home. The drive home was all but silent since the snow was covering the roadway. I did not want to talk because after all children should be seen and not heard, plus I didn't want to disturb Mother while she was trying to concentrate on the roads. Huge snowflakes were falling onto the road and the tree branches, it looked spectacular, like a winter wonderland.

I must have fallen asleep on the drive home because the sound of Gram's garage door opening woke me. "It's about time you woke up!" Mother said. I got out of the car with everyone else and helped unload Gram's suitcases by walking them up to her bedroom. "Thank you, Trisha." Gram said. "You're welcome, Gram. I love you." I whispered as I leaned in and hugged her. "Love you too. Now, do not be long your mother is waiting for you, and you know how she is." Gram said.

The old Cutlas was cold, being it sat at Gram's for a few days while we were helping Kay with her wedding. You could see your breath and the cold brought chills throughout my body. I swear I felt chills in my bones. My teeth were chattering and now I could understand what Lynn left that day mother gave her that cold hose shower on that brisk November day several years prior.

As we were getting out of the car, Mother told me to grab her bags as she began to walk to the trailer ahead of me. I noticed that she stopped midway on the sandstone sidewalk and looked like she was waiting for me. I shut the door and began to walk towards her, heavy the luggage over my shoulder and holding the bookbag with my other hand. When I reached her, I asked if she was okay and that is when she hit me so hard that I lost my footing, falling over the small hillside that was in front of the trailer. My head hit the sandstones as I lost my footing, and I felt a sharp pain in my lip. After I slid down the hill I sat up on my knees and that is when I saw the blood coming from my lip and felt the dual pain in my mouth. The blood began to pour from my lip, I could taste the blood. I put my finger up to my mouth and there my tooth was chipped. I was stunned by what just happened, but not shocked. I was used to this type of abuse, and it would not be normal if something like this didn't happen after I just fucked up once again. It was that night that I started to feel so much hatred towards my mother and father that it felt like it was burning through my soul.

Chapter Sixthteen

Trauma Stricken

AFTER, GROWING UP IN A HOUSEHOLD that believed that sex was love and playing house was normal even if it meant playing with your kids. You learn at an incredibly early age, behaviors, rights, and wrongs or so you should. In a normal well-developed, established, household, fathers do not play with their daughters and call it house. For normal father, their first instinct would be to kill someone who touched a hair on their daughter's head that was sexual or physical. A true bond between parents and their children should be selfless, with an ardent desire to protect their children at all costs, through all aspects of life, mentally, physically, emotionally, and sexually. The way a mother and father reflect upon their paternal instincts helps their children become who they will be later in life. Having a strong paternal instinct helps aid and prepare a child's influence on their work ethic, and resilience, reinforcing the complexities of the world. Children who grow up in abusive households can go one of two directions, become what raised them or become the complete opposite. As for me and my sisters, we became anything but the monsters that once raised us.

By the time I was 15 years old, I had already lost my virginity but in all fairness, I lost that whenever my father decided to molest me at 5 and then continued to playhouse against my will. After a while of being molested and beaten you just get used to it. I remember laying there and counting the blocks repeatedly just to put my mind to another dimension. I would always pretend that I was somewhere else, anywhere, but right there in the moment.

The first time I had sex with someone I was thirteen just a baby. I went camping with a group of my friends and my boyfriend. Of course, Mother and Father did not know I was there, because I had lied and said I was going to my friend Shannon's house, and she said she was going to mine. So, our parents did not suspect a thing. We drank the night away and partied. I thought this was normal behavior being that most of the kids at school partied. Regardless, at least when I was with my friends, away from the house I was not being abused, I was free and able to act like someone my age. I was always so stressed out about being at home. Regardless of the bad choices I made in my personal life, it was not anywhere near as bad as what was happening at home. By now Mother was telling everyone just how badly I was acting out, that I had a horrible problem and was hooked on drugs. That was far from the truth. I had smoked pot once before I reached seventeen, far from the rumors that my mother was viciously spreading which caused my family members one by one to slowly distance themselves from me. It is just what she wanted was for me to become isolated from the world around me, including the most important person in my life, my Gram.

My boyfriend Tony was a real charmer, could convince me to do anything and that is exactly what we did that night. After a night's worth of partying, we climbed into another friend's vehicle, called "The Green Booger." This thing was snot green that all the kids loved to go cruising in. It was the size of a tiny house on wheels, the thing was a beast, and when you started it, I am sure three counties over could hear it. It was not the way I ever pictured losing my virginity, but neither was the other way I officially lost it by being molested. Life was not the same after this. I hit a whole new level of sexual peaking. I went out of control and did not have the best reputation after having sex with Tony for the first time. This was the first time in my life I could say that I had control over my own life. Even if it meant that type of control was a negative response.

In my sophomore year, I met my first serious boyfriend Jer was so kind and caring. He was a dark complexion from his Indian descent, with black hair, deep brown eyes, and glasses.

He was the definition of tall, dark, and handsome. He was not popular by any means, but he could blend in with the crowds. He did play basketball for our high school though, which helped with his confidence and mine if I must be completely honest. It was nice dating someone who was a jock even better to walk around the school like the rest of the kids holding their partner's hand. It was simply amazing to feel normal in my twisted life. Most importantly loved. I felt loved by someone for the first time other than my Gram.

During my sophomore year, I had the pleasure of going to the homecoming like normal teens. I wore a dark green dress with floral designs, a slice up the side, and it made an X in the back area. It was gorgeous and it made me feel beautiful for the first time. My hair was worn up with spirals that came down off to the sides with a rhinestone clip I borrowed from my best friend Anne. Jer wore a matching long-sleeved, a black tie, and black dress pants. We looked like the perfect couple, and we were the perfect couple in our eyes. It did not matter what anyone else said we loved each other.

That night we decided to go on a double date with our friends Stella and Michael. It was the first time I met Michael that he went to another school about 2 hours away. He was a handsome young man, with blonde hair, and blue eyes, and towered over Stella. They too seemed to be the perfect couple complimenting each other in their all-black attire. Instead of going to those fancy steak houses like most kids, we were on a pizza budget and went to Pizza Hut before the dance. We sat and laughed, joking around, to the point of breathlessness. It was one of the best times I ever had as a teenager and still think about it from time to time. I felt beautiful that night and had one of my best friends of all time next to me to experience our first dance together.

On the way to the dance, we were rushing back so we were not late. It was then that the three of us, Jer, Stella, and I started screaming hysterically for Michael to slow the fuck down. Being he was not from the area he didn't realize how fast he was approaching railroad tracks that were notorious for fatal car crashes due to people jumping the tracks at a high rate of speed. Panic-stricken Stella and Jer began to scream even more as I was buckling my seatbelt waiting for impact to happen. It was then I heard Jer and Stella scream, "Jesus fucking Christ we going to die!" Shortly afterward the car goes airborne giving me the sensation of being weightless and completely gravity free from the force of the car hitting the tracks. My seatbelt restricted me from flying forward into Michael, but Jer was not so lucky, he did not have his seatbelt on and landed in between the front and the backseat by the console of the car. The screeching tires could be heard hitting the pavement of the road when the car finally landed back on solid ground. The car fishtailed back and forth to the point I honestly thought Michael was going to roll to the car end over end. It was by the grace of God, that night that the four of us did not end up dead. When we eventually stopped, we stopped in the ditch even though it was not too deep, we became stuck in mud that was caked all around the passenger side tires. Jer and Michael ended up getting it unstuck but that did not go without consequences of front-end damage to the car. Although we knew better as to what happened that night, as far as everyone else went, we lost control, avoiding a deer.

We all danced the night away but did not realize just how precious our time together would be. Stella looked like a beautiful dream girl, her smile big and vibrant, her laugh contagious. She kept pushing her long cherry blonde hair away from her extravagant green eyes. Michael and she complimented each other very well. Young precious love that would once again have a tragic end.

Homecoming came and went causing us all to continue our normal lives the following weeks ahead. Jer and I would walk through the hallways arm in arm, laughing and making jokes as to who loved the other the most. It would not be for several months later that I would find out that I was just a young, dumb, teenager who thought their first love would be forever. Forever just would not be in the cards for me till many years later.

Father and mother during my sophomore year seemed too strangely back off from their tormenting tactics. I'm not sure if it was for the fact they saw my newly formed pride, cockiness, and arrogance grow being too scared to say or do anything that I would let the beans spill about playing house, the beatings, the downright torture, and still having moments of not having much to eat. Or it was the fact that they were now having infidelity issues. It was known around town that mother and father would have friends come from out of town to have orgies. Father was finally satisfied with his liking and expectations, so he began to leave me alone. I think for Mother from day one of their relationship the only reason she was with him was she thought the money he once had would last into their golden years. I could hear the orgy parties they would have after telling me to sleep in their room for the night, which was the furthest room from the living room. I remember one night having to go to the bathroom and creeping through the hallway and hearing how obnoxious their sex party was and the sounds of loud moaning from the sick fucks. I happened to glance through the hallway where I saw Mother riding Father's best friend Tom. That was a site to see. Her oval-shaped body, with rolls bouncing up and down, was quite disgusting, but who am I to judge their barbaric behavior? So, whatever they chose at this point was perfectly fine with me, providing that I was left out of it.

Jer and I were flourishing or so I thought. It was around mid-March close to St. Patrick's Day that I would experience my first heartbreak. Jer stood at the bus stop that day waiting to get on. When I saw him get onto the bus, I scooted over so he could sit with me like he always did but instead, he walked on and passed giving me a sideways smirk. I watched him take a seat on the opposite side of the bus, with another girl named Holly. At first, I thought he needed to talk to her about schoolwork like he had done off and on. However, that was not the case, I could feel the warmth of my face begin as I looked down and saw them holding hands with each other and caressing each other's upper arms. I was pissed beyond ever feeling this way before. I started to shake and cry. I let out a scream and placed my head onto the window crying uncontrollably, not being able to catch my breath, it was then I realized how tight my lungs were becoming. I was in fact in my first asthma attack that I had in a long time. Now I believe years later; it was even an anxiety attack. I was wheezing, trying to take deep breaths, and pretending I was not having this episode in front of the kids who all have called me Trailer Trash at one point in time in their lives. It was then I felt a tight grip on my shoulder as if they were trying to turn me around, but it did not work. There my other best friend Anne sat beside me; her warm arms wrapped around me as she comforted me until we reached school. She kept telling me he was not worth it.

After reaching the school Anne stood up first but held up the line behind her so that I could slide out of my seat first. At this time kids were looking at me, teasing me all over again about Trailer Trash and Junkyard Girl, I began to feel a sense of electricity from the bottoms of my feet to the top of my head. I could not calm down or control myself. I felt the hard tug of someone behind me, but it was Anne, it was Holly. "Hey, bitch you've got a problem with me?" She screamed as I jerked away. I walked off the bus that day unaware of the strength I would find out that I had. As I stepped off the bus that day, I stepped aside throwing my bookbag down and waiting for Holly to get off the bus. Finally, it was her turn, "Why yes bitch I do have a mother fucking problem!" I screamed. I grabbed her from the back and wrapped my hand in her long blonde hair, just like Mother did the day she grabbed ahold of Lynn and cut her hair off, but there were no scissors to cut her hair off. I was about to beat that bitch's ass. I could hear the kids egging on the fight, one screamed, "Catfight." It was then while still holding onto her hair, I grabbed her by her leg picked her up, and body-slammed her to the ground. I could hear another say, "This isn't a cat fight, this bitch is psycho. She is going to fucking kill her." Another one yelled, "Get Trisha off of her." "Dam this is not a catfight! She is beating the fuck out of her. Someone needs to stop her!" One boy yelled. After a while, the cries and pleas began to blend. Finally, Anne began to scream, "Trisha, STOP this right now." It was then and only then I stopped. I got up from being on the ground from us tussling around, Holly was visibly shaken up. As she was slowly getting up from the ground, her white pants were no longer white but caked in mud and leaves. Her blond hair was in a state of disarray being in many directions. Her mouth was bleeding. As she stood slowly, Jer went over to make sure she was okay. It was then she shoved him backward away from her. Teens just stood there and looked at me, not saying a word, or their famous Trailer Trash or Junkyard Girl. It was as if they gained a whole new respect or, they were now afraid of me. Either way, that morning was the last I ever heard them yell those names. Talks about the fight went weeks past that day like I was some superhero to them.

I knew I was in trouble that day, so I walked into the office and opened the door there Jessie sat, our office secretary. "Hey, Trisha what do you need?" She said in a soft-spoken voice. "Well, Jessie I need to speak to Mr. Huggins. I was in a fistfight and want to tell on myself." I spoke in a scared tone of voice. She looked up from what she was doing almost speechless and said, "You were in a fight? That is not like you, Trisha. What happened?" "It was Holy Spencer, she started it by grabbing me and asking what my problem was. I just finished what she started after we got off the bus." I said with my head held down. "Well, you have yourself a seat there Trisha I'll let Mr. Huggins know you're here to see him." She said in a sad voice. "Do you have to tell mother and father?" I asked with tears by now streaming down my face. "Yes, Trisha stuff like this must be reported to the parents involved in the fight. I am sorry that's just how the schools' rules work." "I was afraid of that!" I mumbled while waiting for my fate.

After hearing my side of the story. I was told to sit in the office. As I rounded the side of the wall, Holly sat still crying and wiping her tears away. "Holly, come to my office." Mr. Huggins said in a disappointed tone of voice. I could hear muffled talking but could not make out what was said. After a few minutes, I was called back into Mr. Huggin's office. "Holly and Trisha what you have both done is serious I want you to know you are both suspended for three days with out-of-school suspension. I am sorry to have done this, but you need to have consequences for your actions." Mr. Huggins said in a stern tone of voice. We looked at each other shocked. I figured we would get suspended but how could I explain this to mother and father? They will kick my fucking ass I thought. "Now, go sit in the office and I'll call your parents so they can come and get you." Mr. Huggins said with an annoyed tone of voice. "Mr. Huggins, I promise I will do better. Please do not call my parents." I broke down saying in about the most pathetic tone of voice. It was then that Holly looked over at me and said, "Are you okay? I am sure you will be in trouble, but with the way you are acting is there something else going on?" As she reached over for my hand grabbed it and brought me in closer hugging me. That is right, the very same girl I just beat the shit out had compassion for me. I almost melted into her shoulder standing there holding her. "Trisha, you sure are making a big fuss out of this, now, aren't you?" I was frozen, I could not move. I could not even shake my head to respond. Holly and Mr. Huggins looked at each other and it was then they knew that something was not right at home but couldn't figure out exactly what it was. It was the first time that I ever admitted or gave a hint as to my living situation without saying a word.

Later that night after Father got home, he got the old whiffle ball bat out. It was the first time in forever. "Come here kid, I've got something for you since you want to act like an asshole and can't keep your hands to yourself," Father said. That sounded like the pot calling the kettle black, but who was I to judge? There I stood with my hands against the wall, my legs spread, and shoeless, taking the old position that I had grown all so familiar to take over the years. It was of all things something I did not miss in fact to this day, over 26 years later, I can hear the wiffle ball bat hitting my body from head to the bottoms of my feet. It is a sound I do not think I can ever get out of my head, no matter what I try. I cannot even look at the ones they still sell in the stores without getting anxious and all so familiar sounds playing back in my memories for good old sakes.

Towards the end of the school year, Stella was called to the office during English class over the loudspeaker. She pushed into her chair and grabbed her belongings I think just in case she had to leave to be picked up by someone. As she was about to leave, she looked at me and smiled. I simply waved back. Then, a few moments later she returned bawling, uncontrollably, "Mr. Landon, I need to speak to Trisha." Stella said. Before looking up to see what the problem was, I heard Mr. Landon say, "Are you disrupting my class, Stella?" As he looked up, he could see that Stella could barely stand from crying so much. He rushed over to her, "Are you okay Stella?" All she could do was slide down the wall and shake her head finally blurting out. "No, Michael's dead. He fell asleep last night but did not wake up!" Mr. Landon did not ask who Michael it was obvious that he was Stella's boyfriend by the picture she taped to her book earlier in the school year. I got up and rushed to be beside Stella. "Girls, I think it's best if you both went into this room next to my class so you two could talk." Mr. Landon said. Putting one arm around each of us, he escorted us to the room next door. It was then she explained in more detail that Michael was suffering from headaches and his family would be doing an autopsy on him to determine the cause of death. It would be months later we would learn that Michael had a brain tumor of which he was unaware. Michael was only seventeen when he met his fate.

Chapter Seventeen

The Love Bug Strikes Again

APPROACHING MY JUNIOR YEAR, my depression was in full swing from still dealing with the breakup of Jer and I along with the loss of Michael. So, I began to volunteer at a group home for the MRDD or mentally retarded and developmentally delayed. It would not be until years later I realized just how much I needed these amazing people in my life, to teach me life's lessons through a whole other perspective. To this day I feel blessed to have collaborated with them.

My mother graduated at the end of my sophomore year in nursing and was able to find work in Cadiz at a group home for MRDD. After a few months of her working there I began to volunteer and devote most of my free time to them. The group home housed individuals who had special needs, which were intellectually and developmentally delayed, or impaired from living in a regular household. Some disabilities were mild from being autistic, speech impaired, cognitive, and severe learning disabilities. Others were mute and not capable of speaking, so you had to have patience and figure out what they wanted. Some individuals' disabilities were more severe causing them to have difficulties doing daily activities like bathing themselves or simply walking, causing a couple to need assistance more than others. I almost immediately fell in love with these people and their personalities. I never realized then that they would help me better understand my son I'd have in a few years that was handicapped. I still think it was God's way of helping me in a way I never knew I needed to be helped.

Lisa one of the most wonderful women who inspired me to become the person I am today, was a veteran worker at the group home. She was amazing, her infectious smile showed no connotations or negativity behind it, and she was one of the purest souls one could imagine. Her short platinum blonde hair, against her warm skin tone, highlighted her ocean blue eyes. Lisa also had one of the warmest laughs but was extremely blunt in one of the most loving manners. I would not know at the beginning of our relationship just how much she would mean to me, but she along with her daughter Mandy, and her son La-La his nickname given to him at an early age, would become an instant family to my depleting young life.

It was surprisingly my mother and Lisa's idea to introduce La-La and I after we both had gone through horrible breakups from our first loves or so I thought. The night mother was on her way to introduce us at his house, my stomach was in knots, butterflies even before I laid on him, and Mandy. I wanted to vomit. The country drive to his house was beautiful and reminded me of how my back country road was, it was remarkably similar. Finally, we reached his house it was around 6 pm, it was dark, the fog was incredibly crazy that night, and the moon was full.

Walking to the door, I simply wanted to turn around and leave. To say my nerves were shot would be a true understatement. However, that would have been a huge mistake. It was that night that I met a family that would shortly become part of me. Lisa answered the door, "Well, don't just stand there, come on in!" She said with a smile on her face. I swear that women always had one of the best smiles that I would grow to love and adore. "Thank you, Lisa," I said while stepping into the door. Their home was beautiful, but the love that Lisa had for animals showed. They had a few dogs, and a couple of cats, but in the basement was the biggest surprise, Iggy! He was a 400-pound potbelly pig that acted like it was a guard dog before reaching La-La's room. I could hear the music playing and voices talking. "Well, go on in there," Lisa said. Mandy was standing behind her with a big smile. "Let me go first maybe that will help you relax. Just breathe all will be okay." Mandy reassured me before opening the door. "Are you ready," Mandy asked in an excited tone of voice. "Yes," I said in a whisper as my nervous voice was cracking. The door cracked open and there La-La sat, with his stepsister Kristina, her boyfriend Buddy, and Mandy's boyfriend Edwin. "Well, La-La this is Trisha. Trisha, La-La. This is the rest of the crew." Mandy said as she sat there smoking her cigarette. "Hello, everyone," I said with a shaky voice.

La-La had ice-blue eyes like his mom, her beautiful smile, and bleached blonde hair. He was by far the most beautiful human beginning I had ever laid my eyes on.

The atmosphere was so laid back, nothing like I had ever experienced before. Smoke poured through the room as everyone smoked their cigarettes. His room had black lights in it, causing our teeth to illuminate along with our eyes. The pictures on the walls of mushrooms, flowers, and trolls illuminated from the blacklight, causing all the colors to intensify. The stoner rocker feels, and sound boomed throughout the room.

My people and my people found me. It was by far a young love at its highest point. We were inseparable even though we attended different schools. When I was not at their house, he was at ours, even throughout the week. La-La and his family were my safe place away from the chaos that always seemed to erupt in my house. My mother always had something up her sleeve and ending my happiness was certainly a top priority to her or so it seemed.

Midways through my junior I had gotten a phone call from La-La he was pissed off asking who I was cheating on him with. I had no clue what he was talking about, but that did not matter, the trust was broken and my first love was gone like the wind. I could not talk to him; he wanted nothing to do with anything I had to say. I would go to talk, and he'd interrupt me. It was completely pointless. I had lost the best thing that ever happened to me up to that point. However, there would be more heartache to endure, and it was not letting up. It would not be for a couple of months that I would find out the madness behind my conversation with him. I would like to say I was surprised, but now in my young life, nothing genuinely surprised me anymore.

Although I never once cheated on by him, the sheer disappointment and pain that I was enduring was unbearable and one of the worst forms of pain and betrayal that I ever felt. I was emotionally shattered and felt depleted from my life as I knew it. I walked to the kitchen where Mother had put her pain medicine and looked at the bottle with glossy eyes from all the crying. It was then that I took the remaining bottle of pills placed them in my mouth, and swallowed them.

If the one person I loved the most, who I thought loved me unconditionally could leave me due to hearsay, then I had nothing more to look forward to. I stood there glaring at myself in my mother's make-up mirror she had left on the countertop and threw it causing it to shatter. I did not care though. I had nothing left and I was giving up on the good fight.

I went to bed and closed my eyes. My racing thoughts of how the fuck did he produce this shit to me was over the continued abuse that was happening. I was simply over this horrible deck of cards called life that I was given.

I closed my eyes and prayed God would take me away forever, but that was not the case, and what a disappointment that was when I woke up after 5 pm the following day. To father screaming at me to get my lazy fucking ass up. I kept hearing him say this, but he seemed distant. Come to find out the number of pills I had taken wanting to end my own life, I ended up being severally hungover, to the point I could not walk. I was walking like a town drunk leaving the bar at closing time.

Father was standing in the doorway and for the first time I can say I was lucky that he was there being he caught me from following through the hallway window when I went to walk past him. "Jesus fucking Christ kid, what the fuck are you on?" Father asked in a concerned manner. "Nothing, I am not feeling very well. It is the flu. I am just dizzy." I said while leaning against the hallway wall. I could barely keep my eyes open; it was then I fumbled to the bathroom where I hugged the porcelain God till, I could no longer throw up. It was then I started to become lightheaded, my forehead began to sweat, my vision became blurry, and darkness surrounded me. I passed out once more. I felt like I was at death's door.

I did not have the flu, but I was still feeling the effects of attempting to end my life even several days later. Mother and father never took me to the hospital after I passed out on the bathroom floor. I am sure it was due to the fact of being scared I would talk to the authorities about the abuse. They were not big on doctors or hospitals for fear people would catch on that was not wrapped around their fingers. I sank into a horrible depression deeper than I ever had before.

It was obvious that something was off about me. My dressing attire changed, I started to wear mostly black, skater clothing and turned completely goth. I picked up the nasty habit of smoking. I blended in and looked like kids from the park from years ago. To say my transformation was extreme would be an understatement. Teachers these days would see the obvious change and think that I would need help. However, this was the 1990's and the mental health stigma was not in a full-blown mood during that era.

My junior high year was filled with dark moments that most teens read in the headlines of newspapers or television. It was at these very moments I started questioning if they were even a God. If God were so grand, why would he create so havoc amongst me and my sisters?

I started taking up walking to help with weight loss even though I was not overweight by far. It was my way of mending a broken heart and attempting to help my mental health during the darkest of days, but those dark days were about to get even darker.

I remember sitting in art class it was my one and sometimes the only way to escape the madness that was going on at home. Not sure if Mrs. Palmer ever knew I needed her class for a form of relaxation or not or even how much I looked up to her but one day I pray she realizes the great impact that she had on my life in the most vulnerable times that were circulating around my control. She helped me find my artistic ability I never knew I had before and my love for photography that would help me have my own photography company later in life. I never knew how talented I was in either one until I took her class. I would even go to her class during lunch and study hall just to get away from my innermost demands that plagued my mind.

One by one Mrs. Palmer was taking role calls as to who was there in class, by calling their names. I loved that class; it would be my third year in her class and exploring my artistic ability. It was during my time in her class I discovered my mad photography and artistic ability. They were both something I never knew I could do and had hidden in my back pocket. I would love to believe that my artistic talents came from my Gram who could make anything from her crafts and Aunt Gale who was an insanely talented artist. At one point she even painted Grams old walnut tree and her barn for a Christmas present.

Missy Ash, there was a moment pause, and Mrs. Palmer said her name once more. One girl raised her hand. "Yes, Theresa. How can I help you?" Mrs. Palmer asked. Melissa was in a car accident this morning where she was pronounced dead at the scene. I am so sorry you and the rest of the class must find out this way." Theresa said crying in between tears and the occasional gasping for fresh air. Missy was a beautiful young girl who tried to keep to herself. The jocks would make fun of her for being in the learning disabilities class. I was not friends with her, but the news hit hard. It was the second time that I would have heard about someone so young dying. Who is this God and why is he cruel? I was beginning to lose my hope, faith, and belief in this man I never once met. This would not be the last tragic moment that would hit my life before I graduated, and it certainly would not be the last of the series of earth-shattering events.

Chapter Eighteen

My Senior Year

I WOULD LIKE TO SAY THAT ENTERING my senior year life was about to change for the better but that would not be the case for this plagued life I was leading. In July of 1997, a group of my friends and I would go celebrate the 4th of July. I, Linda, Elizabeth, and Jessica would ride in one truck while Linda's boyfriend Josh and his brother Jacob would meet us at the fair. For some of us, it was the first time getting out and kicking our shoes off, and for those, it would be the first and last of the high school outings as they knew it.

That day was extremely long, temperatures were soaring into the upper nineties, with the blazing sun giving us no end in sight of the slightest hint of clouds to give us the slightest of coverage, so the mugginess was awful and breathtaking, and it started with my softball game being a doubleheader. Which meant playing two ball games against the same team back-to-back. Our teams had to take extra precautions to stay cool by taking cool breaks by dipping our towels into coolers of ice and placing them on our necks and foreheads. It felt like the fire depths of hell taking over the world consuming us from the outside in.

During the game, a friend asked me if I wanted to see fireworks and spend the night, and I decided to go. Besides, it was a fantastic way to get out of the house and away from the monsters that called themselves mother and father.

After the games, I was completely exhausted and decided to take a nap. During that time, I kept having a continuous dream of being in a vehicle and seeing lights behind us rolling, as if you would take a flashlight and move your hand in circles. I could hear screaming and kept seeing feet under a vehicle. None of this made sense until later that night. I would wake up, go back to bed and continue my dream right where it left off. It was so realistic, that each time I'd wake up I would be drenched in sweat, shaking, and my heart racing merely feeling like I was about to have a heartache.

Just as I was putting the last curl into my hair, I heard Linda's truck pull in and the sound of her horn. I always had my friend beep when they would pick me up, I never wanted anyone to see the inside of the trailer and how deplorable the conditions were. I was ashamed, embarrassed, and humiliated enough when the bus would show, there was no way in hell I would allow anyone inside, except one person who was La-La.

As I was making my way to her truck a snake slithered a crossed my foot going under the trailer. It was common to see snakes in the summer daily, being father had his junkyard and that is where most of the snakes loved to lay. I often wondered if the snakes were that bad if there were any inside the trailer.

"Hey, chick thank you for picking me up! I wish I could drive, but you know how mother and father are!" I said in a matter-of-fact voice. "Yeah, for sure. They need to get over themselves and allow you to get your driver's license for Christ's sake!" Linda said with a disgusted tone of voice as she was back out of the driveway. "I know, it's just one more way of them trying to control me and keep me at the house!" I said in an annoyed voice gritting my mouth together.

On our way to pick Jessica up Linda and I were brainstorming on who else we could invite to see fireworks and hang out. That is when we thought about Elizabeth, she was a shy, backward girl, who was a band member, of the American Honors Society, and Future Teachers of America. She was one of the smartest girls I knew and looked up to her. Once we picked Jessica up, we ran past the thought of stopping at Elizabeth's house to see if she could go. Of course, being we were all friends it was perfectly fine with Jessica. I always loved hanging out with these two girls but a strain in the relationship was about to happen for an event that nobody could have foreseen, or could we?

The three of us girls stood at the door of Elizabeth anxious for someone to answer. Finally, she came to the door, "Hey, ladies what are you all too?" Elizabeth said with a warm smile on her face simultaneously we said, "Do you want to see fireworks tonight? We are on our way there and would love for you to go!" "Girls, I'm not sure about tonight I'm pretty tired this weather is just draining me!" Elizabeth said. "PLEASE!!" We said in a beggingly manner. She stood there apprehensively and finally said she would ask her parents. "Mom, Dad, can you please come here?" Elizabeth asked. They peered around the corner from their kitchen and at first, they too, said no. "You never let me do anything! I am a senior and never get to do anything!" Elizabeth said with an annoyed tone. I'm not sure if it was the fact we all put her parents on the spot or not, but they said she could go.

The truck was cramped not a lot of room to move around in, Jessica and I sat in the bucket seats which faced each other while Elizabeth had the honor of sitting in the front seat. She would not have been able to sit in the back anyways being how tall she was. So, we were glad to sit in the back seat. The music was loud, and Linda the speed demon was driving, I am not sure if she even knew what the brake was used for especially around turns, and her driving always scared me the shit out of me. If you would ever ask her to slow down, her reply would always be, "Speed up? Sure thing!" So, after some time I stopped asking her to slow down because it was not my vehicle, nor a ticket I would get, and most of the time she was one of only three of my friends who drove. I did not want to jeopardize not having rides from point A to B!

The smell of fresh popcorn filled the air, along with kids screaming from being on the rides. The garden light illuminated the walkways and Christmas lights hung above. The Ferris wheel seemed massive with its flashing lights as it was going around and round. It was so crowded that it was hard to walk so we decided to make our way home. Just as we were walking to the truck, we heard pop-pop, a clown stood, and the balloon he was blowing up ended up popping. I jumped and began to shake. "Trisha, what's wrong, are you okay?" Elizabeth asked. "Yeah, yeah, sorry that just caught me off guard," I said with a fake smile.

Once we got to the trucks Jacob and Josh were already standing by Josh's matching ranger that Linda had. We mingled for a while trying to figure out what we were going to do, it was simply too crowded and hot to be around that many people. That is when we all decided to go back to Linda's house. On the drive there we had the music cranked up, singing to every song that came onto the radio that day. We were having the time of our lives and could not ask for better company.

Pulling into Linda's house we noticed her parents' car was not there and thought how strange that was. We could hear Ace barking; it was their German Shepard who only could be described as a beast with his massive weight and height. He was solid black and although he looked mean, was the biggest lap dog.

After we made our way into the house and began to settle down, Linda got a phone call saying that her dad was in the hospital with food poisoning. Being young, dumb, and without a care in the world, we all got the brilliant idea to have a bonfire at Josh and Jacob's house. At first, I went to get into the truck with Josh, Jessica, and Elizabeth, but then I got out and decided to allow Elizabeth to ride with them, by splitting the six of us up I could stretch my legs out in the backseat. Linda, Jocab, and I pulled out first then Josh would follow behind. Not long after that I got the worst feeling in the world as I turned around and looked behind us and that is when I saw their headlights, rolling, as if you would take a flashlight and move your hand in circles. "Linda, turn the fuck around they just wrecked!" I screamed in terror. I just kept screaming repeatedly. Panic-stricken Linda found the first driveway to turn around at and speed back.

We could see the headlights in the distance facing upward against the tree line when we started to approach the accident scene. The truck barely came to a stop when I pushed my door open and began to run over the hillside. Josh came flying up over the hill, out of breath, then collapsed onto the driveway. "Where the fuck are the girls, Josh?" I screamed, but he was no help.

The area where the truck landed was full of brier bushes and thickets, Jessica was lying on the ground screaming in pain, but Elizabeth was nowhere to be found. She was not in the truck or around it. "Jessica, where's Elizabeth? Where's Elizabeth Jessica?" I screamed in the utmost panic-stricken voice. "I do not know. She helped pull me from the truck and that was the last I saw of her." Jessica screamed. Then, I saw it, there Elizabeth's shoe was sticking out from under the truck. I climbed under screaming, "Elizabeth, talk to me! Are you okay?" Not a word was whispered back, there she was motionless. Then I finally heard a gasp. I started clearing her airway out and removing the debris from around her mouth, nose, and face. "Are you okay?" I asked. "Yeah, I think so," Elizabeth said in between from pain. "Can you feel your legs, Elizabeth?" I yelled, praying that she could be in a fetal position and the frame of the truck was on her. "Yes, I can." She said in between gasps.

What seemed to take forever, the squad finally showed up and made me leave Elizabeth so they could tend to her. "It is all your fault, Josh! You should not have been driving that fucking fast. If she dies, I will kill you myself!" I screamed. He just stood frozen, not saying a word, not moving, crying, and screaming. Off in the distance, the moon was shining brightly from the partial lunar eclipse called the Waxing Crescent Phase that was happening. The eerie feel was not explainable and haunts me to this day.

We sat in the hospital so silent you could hear a pin drop. Linda's dad and her mom sat there with disgust, to say they were angry would be an understatement. "So, you guys decided to take my food poisoning as an advantage and wanted to go back to Josh and Jacob's house for a bonfire." He eventually said. "Yeah." Linda and I said in a whispering manner. He just sat there glaring at us, not saying anything, but if looked could kill we would most certainly be dead.

What seemed to take an eternity was Jessica's mom came through the doors carrying a picture. Here was an ultrasound picture of Jessica's baby. They were healthy and nothing wrong with either, except a couple of bruises here and there from the rolling truck and her being tossed into the grass by Elizabeth right before the truck rolled back onto her.

Elizabeth was not so lucky both her mom and dad were explaining that when the truck landed back on top of it, fractured three vertebra and she would need life flighted to Cincinnati Children's Hospital for emergency surgery. The news hit all of us in diverse ways some were crying, screaming, anxious, worried, and as for me I was all the above and began to withdraw from the rest of the group of people. My heart rate began to race, my palms began to sweat along with my forehead, and I began to throw up, barely making it to the bathroom.

A loud noise of screaming erupted in the waiting room, there Jacob and Josh's dad stood, screaming at the boys saying it was all their fault because of the accident. That is when he drew back and punched Josh in the face. Linda's dad jumped up and pushed their dad backward. "ENOUGH! You do not think that he does not already have guilt for what just happened?" The last thing they need is this." He screamed.

One by one we began to leave the hospital but not before Elizabeth was transported by emergency helicopter. I could hear the helicopter making the noise of a vortex of air generated by the main rotor, whirling, whirring, and chopping loudly above the hospital as they began the flight to Cincinnati.

I called my mother begging her to pick me up from Linda's house, as horrible as my home life was, I simply wanted to be in my bed to process what just happened. I had racing thoughts and every time I attempted to close my eyes all I could see was the lights going into a circle like a flashlight that was going into circles. It was around 4:30 am when I called home, mother had answered very pissed off because I woke them. "Mother, there has been an accident. Elizabeth is on her way to Cincinnati's Hospital they believe her back is broken. I just want to come home." I screamed in a begging voice. "You called me for this shit? You fucking woke me for this?" Mother screamed. Then I heard what no child wants to hear when all they want is for their mother to simply be a mother, drop what she was doing even if it meant, throwing her fucking shoes on at 4:30 in the morning, and taking a drive to pick her panic-stricken daughter up. Click! "Hello, mother? Mother, are you there?" I said while crying into the phone. There was dead silence, she was not there, in fact, she had hung up on me when

I needed her the most. Thinking she accidentally hung up, I redialed the number. Ring, ring, ring, "WHAT?" Mother screamed. Hello mother, you accidently hung up on me. Can you please pick me up?" I whispered, trying not to wake anyone. "NO! Goodnight, Trisha." Mother screamed. It was then I realized she did not accidently hang up, but deliberately hung up on me. I sat there in Linda's room, crying, I was short of breath, my chest was hurrying, and my body was rocking back and forth. I was all along.

No matter how much I attempted to sleep the moment I closed my eyes I kept reliving the night's tragic events all over again. It would not be till years later that I would be diagnosed with PTSD or Post Traumatic Stress Disorder from that night along with my childhood abuse. I would relive that night in my dreams and through flashbacks when I would drive around a turn that looked like an accident scene. The worst part was living with the terrible feeling of guilt and distressing thoughts that would torment me for years to come.

Finally, I decided to get up and walk home. I did not care how pissed off mother and father would be, I just wanted to be home, and in my bed. I walked for 2 hours that morning before I reached home. Once I reached my bed, I collapsed and cried even more.

That morning hell would break loose yet again when mother and father realized that I walked over ten miles to come home, and I did not wait for someone to give me a ride home. I heard the door creeping open and there my mother stood. I sat up in bed, barely able to keep my eyes open. "Who brought you home, it's not even 8 am." She snapped. "I could not sleep and was having nightmares every time I would close my eyes. I walked home." I said as I was almost falling back to sleep from the sheer exhaustion of what just transpired. "You fucking bitch, you could fucking wait till someone could bring you home? You fucking walked?" She screamed as she headbutted me. If waking me was her goal I was awake at that point and pissed. "Yes, I fucking walked home, now what are you going to do about it?" I screamed. It was then she drew her hand back and slapped me a crossed my face. The burning sensation was the same sensation I felt many times before. I was simply used to it and did not react. All I wanted was to be left the fuck alone.

Elizabeth sustained three vertebras which were broken, rods in her back, and was diagnosed with being permanently paralyzed for the rest of her life. She would have to live in a wheelchair for the rest of her life. The community came together including a local construction company that built a new porch deck to make it easier to have access coming and going. There would be donation cans that were placed at local businesses and even a benefit. Our little community pulled together for Elizabeth and her family.

Our summer went fast that year and soon it was the first day of my senior year. After homeroom, all staff and students would be called into the auditorium and that is when I'd hear about more tragic news. Mr. Huggins began to speak, "Welcome back students and staff to our 1997-1998 school year. I hope your summer was filled with happy memories with your families. With the news of Elizabeth Hauber being in a tragic accident that caused her to become paralyzed. We will have school counselors available for our staff and students. Also, we learned that Mason Creston was found dead today at his home. We do not have any other news currently. We at Jewett-Scio High School are so sad that we must tell you all this tragic news. I sat there crying and speechless, Stella's brother was dead, he was gone and not coming back. I would no longer see him walking the halls and coming up behind me tugging at my bookbag as he would tease me oh so often.

Chapter Nineteen

Accountability and Responsibility

AFTER THE TRAGIC EVENTS UNFOLDED one by one in my junior and senior year of high school, I started walking to relieve my mind of the utter torment of reliving the accident, in my dreams and seeing it through flashbacks. I was simply trying to be human and live a normal life. Since the accident all my friends went their separate ways and did not stay in contact with each other. I am not sure if that were from the guilt we all shared or the fact we couldn't face each other without arguing about who was to blame for that night. After this much tragedy, it could not get any worse, right? I could not be more mistaken!

I was sitting in my room as I often did to drown out the world around me from hell, I was living by listening to the radio. "Trisha, can you come here?" I heard Mother ask but pretended I did not hear her. I could not stand being around her let alone talking to her. It seemed that anything that ever came from that hateful woman's mouth was to hurt me in her abusive ways. "Trisha, turn that fucking radio down. Get out here!" Mother screamed. I turned the radio down and walked to the living room where she sat like always smoking her cigarette and blowing it out the window. "Hey, guess who's having a baby?" she said with a half smirk and half smile. My sister Kay and Ryan were having infertility issues attempting to get pregnant, they would either miscarry or have a tubal pregnancy causing them to have to abortion. There was no in-between or full-term pregnancy yet. "I have no idea, mother. Are Kay and Ryan pregnant? Will this pregnancy stick?" I asked in a concerned tone of voice. "No, La-La and his new girlfriend. They just found out. She is around 3 months." She said in a confused tone of voice. "What, La-La?" I said, in a tone to reassure myself that what I heard was not happening. "Yes, do you know another La-La? She asked with the biggest smirk. I had no control, I lost control at that very moment and dropped to the floor in a fetal position and screamed. I knew right there that there would be no chance of us ever getting back together. He was too family-orientated due to his parents being divorced. He would never do that to his child. "What the fuck is wrong with you?" She screamed telling me to get up and get out of her face.

"What the fuck is wrong with her? What the fuck is wrong with you?" I heard Father yell. It was then that I felt a tug on my shirt, "Come on kid. Get up and go to your room. It will be okay!" Father stood over me, nudging me. I could not move, I could not breathe, I just lay there. It was then that father bent down, picked me up, and carried me to my bedroom. "Kid you'll be okay," Father said as he closed the door behind him.

I just lay there motionless but could hear the screams of Father saying how selfish Mother was for telling me about La-La. "What it's not like they were getting married!" She snapped. "Candy you better shut the fuck up!" Father screamed.

I could not take it anymore, I grabbed my tennis shoes, threw them on told Father I was going for a walk, and left. I heard mother say, "Get the fuck back here." However, I ignored the bitch and walked out.

I reflected on life a lot during my walk. I thought about the shitty cards that were dealt to my sisters and myself at such an early age, between the verbal, mental, physical, starving, and sexual abuse I'm not sure which one I'd say was worse. Mother was the best manipulator, narcissistic, and soulless person I ever knew. She was extremely smart and knew how to get into someone's head, playing with them like a game of cat and mouse. The psychological trauma that we endured lasted into our adulthood for each of us girls. Those bruises were just a temporary reminder of what was. I thought about the abuse that both mother and father put Lynn through especially, that day when she hosed her off in the middle of November, then saw her previous bruises on top of bruises, her vertebrae showing, along with her ribs. I still had not forgiven myself for the fight that I had gotten into with Lynn from that day either. I can make the excuse and lie saying that I was so young that I did not know better. The fact of the matter was I knew better. I targeted Lynn that day because she was the weakest of the two of us. I beat on her because that is what I wanted to do to mother and father that day, but knew they always had the upper hand. I used her pushing mother off the porch as an excuse to finally lose my shit on someone and come unglued.

I knew what mother and father were doing to all of us was simply wrong. I started catching on as a child, especially after becoming friends with Annie. I saw what her family was like, nothing like mine. I mean what family does not have issues, but to me her family was my safe- haven. Annie knew stuff was happening, but she kept her word and did not breathe it to anyone.

I will never forget the first time; I went to Annie's house. We sat at their kitchen table eating dinner like a real, normal family would. I was in third grade when I went to their house to visit for the first time. We had homemade buttered noodles, BBQ chicken, and corn. I never had BBQ chicken until that day. I was picking around it, too scared not to eat for fear I would get into trouble and too scared not to eat being I was not sure when I would eat again. Annie's sitter sat there and teased me saying that if I did not eat all my food, I would have to hear about the starving children in Africa. If Jenny only knew that I too was starving from time to time.

My mind was racing, seeing all these tragic, uneventful, events that had occurred during my whole life. My life was flashing before my eyes. I could not take it anymore and let out this terrifying scream, a scream that I had never let out before, at a pitch that I never knew existed. I was letting all my emotions out at once. I saw the first time I was raped, my Strawberry Shortcake nightgown, The Wizard of Oz, my sticky hand, the hanging the day Lynn and I were only playing but got blamed. I saw the Halloween Party of 1986, Butch, Gram, Pap, Kay, the turkey flying out the backdoor, Jer, the first time I met Mandy, La-La, Lisa, and the crew, and the tragic accident with Elizabeth. I was spirally out of control, but I was the only one who could control my actions, my accountability, and my responsibility for events that I could have prevented but chose not to for fear of my father shooting my family. It was the first time in my life that I realized that I simply could have been a better person, La-La would still be with me and the baby that was on its way could've been ours together so I could love unconditionally and be loved.

My whole body was trembling, and snot, and tears, were draining from my face. It was a horrible sight to see. I did not care that when people were driving by, they saw the madness unfolding, I did not care that I was talking to myself and screaming at the heavens about how unfair all our lives were. I simply did not have two fucks to give.

As I was making my rounds around town doing my usual walk, I was beginning to walk down High Street, then there was an old familiar face standing on their porch smacking two rugs together. I could not believe my eyes, it was the dust from the rugs, causing me to see things. It could not be, it is not, but it indeed was Lynn. As I was approaching, I thought I would just walk by that she did not want to see me anyhow after all the horrible things I said, and did, to her as a kid. Then, it happened I looked up, locking in on her deep brown eyes, and she was locked onto mine. I wanted to stop, but should I? I wanted to beg for forgiveness, but would she forgive me? There was only one way to find out. "Hello, Lynn?" I said as I am pretending that I was only going to say that in passing. "Hello, Trisha. How are you doing girl, get on up here and see your old sister!" Lynn said excitedly. I didn't know what to say or how to say all the things that I wanted to tell her over these years.

When I finally reached her, I collapsed into her extended arms and began to bawl. "I am so sorry Lynn for everything I put you through. I am so sorry, I was so mean, hurtful, and hateful to you. Please forgive me!" I said while sobbing into her shoulder. There was a moment of silence I did not think she heard me nor could understand me. "Lynn, did you hear me?" I finally mustered up enough courage to ask her. Lynn practically had to peel me off her. Then, she took her hand and brought my chin upward so I could see her. "There is nothing to forgive, Trisha. Do you hear me? Do you understand? Nothing to forgive! You were just a little girl. I love you." Lynn said.

Lynn invited me inside and we talked for hours catching up. She had told me about her daughter whom she carried until 7 months, but she tragically passed away due to the same heart condition Lynn had. We talked about the abuse all of us girls endured and compared stories, which was the first time that ever happened. I told her about my ex-La-La and how he and his girlfriend were expecting, how mother rubbed it in my face. I told her every detail about my life since the last day I saw her. It felt great catching up, talking to her, feeling her touch, and simply hearing her voice again.

As I was getting ready to leave her husband Michael walked in the door. "What are you of all people doing here?" He said in a stern tone of voice while giving me a dirty look over the top of his coke bottle glasses. "I am sorry I was just leaving. I should not have stopped." I said in a nervous tone. "You're God dam right you shouldn't have stopped!" He screamed. "I am sorry Lynn I did not mean to cause any trouble. Thank you for talking to me. I love you!" I said in a quick tone all in one breath. "I love you too Trisha!" Lynn said. I shut the door and began walking down the steps when I heard Michael say, "That bitch better never come back, or I'll give her something she'll regret!" That day I knew I would never see Lynn again, not in passing, not to visit, because I wanted to do the only thing, I could do at that point I wanted to give her peace and not have to live on eggshells for fear of her husband walking into the house and seeing me, causing her more trouble. I heard through the grapevine years later that he along with her second husband beat on her. I am not sure if Lynn ever knew a normal life outside of abuse and tragic events. This statement right here just broke my heart to think that Lynn never knew true love, comfort, and warmth from another human being. Lynn never knew what a normal, safe, healthy relationship was with anyone.

Chapter Twenty

Finally Someone to Love Me

PANIC-STRICKEN, I knew what was about to come next. I yelled at my attacker, to get off me, I was pregnant, but that did not matter to him. I felt the pull of my hair, his smelly breath, as he was yelling at me, and smashing my head against the floor. Just when I thought I was about to pass out. I heard a voice saying, "Don't give up! Get up!" When I saw my opportunity, I hit him as hard as possible. He got off me gasping for air. There was only one way out, down the hallway to the back door. The only problem was there were no steps, I would have to jump. I was five months pregnant visibly showing. It was like I either jumped or I was going to die right then and there. I heard the pounding of his footsteps and him yelling, "Hey, kid, where do you think you're going you little bitch"! It was right then that I jumped. I felt a pain in my stomach, but ran to my car, and left. Not long after, I finally braved enough courage to look up in the rearview mirror to see if he was behind me. The coast was clear, there were no signs of my father.

There was no sense in the madness that surrounded the events that day other than I had come home later than expected the night before due to money being missing from the cash register. I was working in Cadiz at the time at a little grocery store called Farm Fresh as a clerk and still working at the group home. I was determined to give my son everything that I never had, so working hard to buy his crib, clothes, and diapers were my priorities. The night before Father chased me down and beat the ever-living fuck out of me, our registered had come up short and we could not figure out why. We counted the money that night several times until I finally pulled the drawer and saw the missing $110 lying underneath. It was getting later than usual and typically I would be home shortly before midnight. However, that was not the case, I did not get home till after 12:30 AM. When I walked in, I thought I was being quiet enough not to wake Father, but that was not the case. I slowly shut the door and began to walk past Father, laying on the couch but decided to get water to take to bed. After becoming pregnant I was always so thirsty and wanted to drink if I woke up. Just as I was walking past the TV and started into the hallway I heard, "Thanks for waking me, kid. Why the fuck are you coming in so fucking late? Being a whore again? Oh, that is right you are already pregnant!" Father yelled. "I am sorry I did not mean to wake you. The cash register came up short and we had to figure out where the money went." I whispered in an attempt not to wake my mother too. "Yeah, right, what the fuck ever! Get the fuck out of my face!" Father snapped.

I could not get comfortable that night. I had found out only three months after graduation that I was pregnant, a complete surprise. However, I was bound and determined to be the best mom possible. After all, I'd never want to be the same type of parent I grew up with. The day I found out I was pregnant I wasn't feeling well at all. Never expecting to be pregnant I decided to take a test just in case. It turned positive immediately. I was shocked, scared, somewhat disappointed in myself, but happy all in the same sense. Sadly, my pregnancy would be short-lived carrying the baby to only 22 weeks.

My feet were swollen, and my stomach was sore. I finally fell asleep after 3 am but like before I was having a continuous dream. I wake up in a sweat and go back to sleep. The dream was eerie, I could see the waist of a woman, her pushing to give birth, then a doctor holding a baby girl up, saying, "It's a girl." This happened numerous times that night. Then, I would wake up. At 7:23 am I woke up to the bed being wet, my water had. I was twenty-two weeks pregnant, but the sense of calmness I had was remarkable. I got up, went to the bathroom and saw blood on the toilet paper. The blood was a very bright red, thick and heavy. I hurried up and got dressed to drive to the hospital. Father was sitting on the couch, "Where are you going?" Father asked. "I am miscarrying. I am going to the hospital. I will be back." I said with a matter-of-fact tone of voice." I reached for my keys that were by the front door. "Do you...." Father started to say. "Not." I opened the door and left.

The hospital was over 45 minutes away in Martin's Ferry. As I was driving, I was pulled over because I was going, over 70 in a 55. "Why aren't you in a hurry young lady?" The police officer said. "Yes, I am. I am having a miscarry and I am on my way to the hospital." I said with a panic-stricken voice. "I'm sorry to hear that I'll alert the others that you're coming through with your four ways on and what's happening." The police officer said. "Okay, have a great day!" I said while peeling out.

Right before the group home, I noticed that my gas light came on and although I had my purse, payday was not until the following day. I had no choice but to stop and ask my mother for gas money. The day was cold I could see my breath as I was approaching the group home. I opened the door and one of the residents was standing there, "Hi, Trisha! What are you doing here? It is your day off!" He said with excitement. "Hello, James. Where is the mother?" I asked anxiously. I bet that was the first day I was ever happy to see her. "She is in the nurse's office. Here I will take you." He grabbed my hand and led the way.

Mother was sitting in her chair, getting the resident's medicine ready to pass out. She looked up and peered over the top of her glasses. "What are you doing here, so early? You do not work today!" Mother said. "I need gas money. I am going to the hospital. I am having a miscarry!" I said while tears streamed down my face. Mother stopped dead in her tracks.

"How do you know? What is happening?" Mother asked. I explained that morning that I had woken up to my bed being wet. By this time too, I started to have sharp pains in my stomach. Lanna, a worker came in and asked if I was okay because she overheard what I was saying. She and I were becoming best friends at the time. "I just need gas money so I can go to the hospital," I said in a matter-of-fact tone of voice. "Well, I cannot leave now, and you don't need to drive to the hospital by yourself. Wait for me while I get the resident's medicine passed and I will drive you down." Mother said.

It seemed like Mother took her sweet old time, not really having a care in the world, not rushing, not panicking, just being slower than normal. It was like she was enjoying the fact that I was about to lose my child. The one person I could completely love without strings attached and I could break the chains of abuse my son Matthew!

The drive there was long, winding curves, as I would always say they were the kiss-your-ass good-bye turns if an accident were ever to occur. The road was just awful. Midway there I began to throw up into a grocery store bag. The smell made me want to continue to get sick. Mother was going well over the speed limit by now, but still able to maintain control over her car, throughout the sharp turns. We finally reached the hospital, it was around 10 in the morning, snowflakes began to fall, the wind started to pick up, and the snow was dancing.

I was admitted to the hospital immediately and set to labor and delivery. It was then the doctor confirmed my suspicions that I was indeed in labor. Matthew would be making his way sometime that day. "I am sorry Trisha, but there is nothing we can do. "You're only 22 weeks gestational and babies typically don't live when they're delivered this early." The doctor said he was putting his head down in the sense that he too was upset. I could not hold it back when the tears began to flow, and I let out this barbaric scream. I did not care who heard me, I didn't care who I upset, all my emotions came out in one scream. I was pissed, enraged, and shocked. There was nothing I could do I would have to lay through labor and delivery only to watch my lifesaver die before my eyes. "

There was a knock on the door with an old familiar face, it was Lanna. "How are you feeling?" She asked with tears streaming down her face. Before I could say a word, she wrapped her arms around me and placed her right hand on my stomach. "I am so sorry Trisha. I am so sorry!" Lanna said hysterically. She was one of only three friends that would visit that day, beside Aunt Tillie. Lanna sat beside me rubbing my hand and reassured me. Occasionally, would say how sorry she was.

Mother had stepped out of the room; I could hear her on the phone. She was talking to Kay at the time, explaining that I was in the hospital and that Matthew would be here anytime. It was then I heard her say, "Kay, are you serious? Are you sure? Is that truly happening?" It was not until after I'd had Matthew did that I learned what the conversation was about.

A nurse came in to take my vitals and was sitting beside me talking about how she had just recently lost her child. She explained that there were counselors that I could talk to and other staff members. The nurse also said that there was a team of doctors and nurses that were flying in from Columbus to do everything they could do to save my baby.

It was then that I felt pressure, and something hit my inner thigh. It was wet, foreign, and moving. Matthew was coming regardless of whether we were ready or not. I reached between my legs and felt his leg on mine. I pulled my hand back shocked. Then, told the nurse to check me. "Do not push. Whatever you do, do not push!" The nurse said as she was running out of the room. My doctor ran in and checked me, while my mother stood at the bottom of the bed leaning against the wall. "Trisha your baby is breech. We are going to have to turn him. Do not push." The doctor said in a monotone voice. The nurse came over and began to rub my stomach forcefully attempting to turn him and did this for several minutes. Nothing they were doing did any good. Matthew was coming and he was coming breeched. A few pushes later he was born, he let out a faint cry as the doctors carried him away onto his table to begin putting a breathing tube into his throat. The doctors and nurses tried so hard to make sure that he would have a fighting chance. After several minutes the doctor and nurses told me what I already knew that there was nothing they could do. I just sat in there in silence, crying, and shaking my head.

I remember the nurse who brought Matthew over, was teary-eyed as she placed him into my arms. He had all ten toes, although he was born with a clubfoot, ten fingers, beautiful blonde hair, and the most adorable button nose like mine. He looked just like his father who was all but a distant memory at this point. I held this precious angle until he took his last breath. The doctors medicated me so much though I could not understand why his mouth kept coming up and I'd push it back shut. One of the worst feelings in the world is watching the only soul that I gave unconditional, endless love pass away in my arms. He was now in the arms of the angels.

Lanna, Aunt Tillie, and Mother all took turns holding him. Each one said something special to his sweet innocent little boy. Then, it was time for the nurse to take him away in preparation for the funeral the next day.

As Mother was getting ready to leave, she knelt and hugged me. I am quite sure it was due to people being around and wanting to put on the show of being a concerned mother. As she was pulling away, I said, "I'm so glad Kay didn't have to go through this!" As I was gasping for air in between tears. That is when she looked at me, pushed my hair off my forehead, and said, "You don't have to worry now you're an aunt!" I paused for a second, confused with the words that just came out of her mouth. "What do you mean I'm an aunt now? How did having my son cause me to become an aunt?" I said once more in between breaths. "Kay's doctor delivered a healthy baby girl this morning. Her mother worked at Hooters and walked in from her shift, delivered her, and left. I was not going to tell you because of the circumstances but since you brought it up." She said with a half smirk.

All I could think about was the conversation we had the day I found out I was pregnant. I called my mother from my friend's house and told her. That is when she said, "What do you think Kay will do at Christmas time next year when you have a baby and the baby, she longed for won't be?" Mother said screaming angrily through the phone. I sat in silence not saying a word, but all I could think of now was, that I would be the one at Christmas time without a baby, while Kay would have hers.

Later, that night the nurse came into my room handing me a large yellow envelope. "What's this?" I asked with a puzzled voice. "This is Matthew's paperwork, his height, weight, footprint, it was all there, including his tiny measuring tape." She said then patted me on my leg and walked out.

A brief time later I heard another knock on the door, it was another nurse who needed to check my vitals. I sat there in silence just staring at the television. "Okay, honey is there anything I can get you? How about your baby, I can bring it in if you want!" The nurse said with a smile. It was then I looked at her and said, "Well, if you would have looked at my chart you would have seen that my son Matthew died this morning. Get the fuck out!" I said in an angry voice. "Oh, sweetie I am so sorry. I did not know!" She spoke in an embarrassed tone. The door closed behind her and thankfully I did not see her again that night.

Both my friends Arik and Ria showed up at the hospital later that night, not knowing what to say. Especially my best friend Ria, who was expecting any day. She became so distraught that she went into labor that night laboring for four long days until her precious baby girl was born. We had been friends since first grade and did everything together, including getting pregnant. One time during our sophomore year we decided to wear sailboat shirts and flannels, and then I made a big deal about us always matching when she got on the bus. I was going through so much at home that I lashed out at her, although it was both of our ideas to match. She will never know just how much she means to me. To this day she is still my best friend. It is friendships like hers that truly have meant the world to me, even now in times when the world is crashing down.

Once everyone left and the shock started to wear off, I called Mother to see if she was coming back to the hospital like she had promised. It was not the answer that I wanted. She told me she was too exhausted and would not be back till tomorrow when I needed to be picked up. I did everything to try to get her to spend the night, but the answer was always no. I simply needed my mother that night, but truly she could not be there.

It was Gram and mother who came to the hospital picking me up so I could attend Matthew's funeral. I remember the long drive home that seemed to be even longer that day. Gram let me sit in the front seat of her car, while mother was driving. I had no control, the medicine they gave me was tampering off and the realization of going home without my son, my first person to love, and be loved conditionally was gone. I would never be able to touch him or hold him again. Those few months I carried him, getting to know his every kick, and movement, our time to bound, was over.

There was a small group of immediate family members that stood at the graveside that day. His casket was donated by the local funeral home because that is what they simply did. They told mothers they did not feel right for taking money for babies to be buried. His casket was so small, a foot long perhaps, it was pearly white, with iridescent angles on it which glistened in the sunlight that day was buried with my Pap! After so long I simply responded he died, is there anything else you want? I could not manage it anymore, the longer the day the ruder I got. I went to my boss and told her I had to leave. She completely understood and told me to take the following day off too.

Instead of driving directly home, I took a detour out by Tappan Lake, I was raging, hysterical, and pissed off at the world. I kept hearing my mother's voice say, "For a baby to be born, a death must occur. It was a phrase she had said over the years. I wondered why Matthew and my niece Heather could both be born healthy at full term. I am not sure why my mother always thought that, but it made me extremely bitter and angry with God. I hated God for taking my son, for taking the one person I could love unconditionally, and be loved by. I wanted nothing more than to be with Matthew. I had nothing else to live for. I wanted to die and be with him. I wanted to hold my baby again.

I turned the radio up and took my seatbelt off. I was crying so much I could not see the road; my vision was blurry; my body was trembling. I was losing control in a way I have never lost control before. I was going home to see my son. Coming around the bin was a semi a big eighteen-wheeler, I put my head back and closed my eyes. I could hear the screeching of tires and my body letting go. It was then I saw Matthew, but he was not a baby, he was in his later years, his late twenties. "Mom, it's not your time! Go home!"

About The Author

Trisha McAfee-May grew up with her sisters Stephanie and Tracy in the backwoods of Ohio in a poor family. She struggled most of her life with trying to fit in because of being poor, living in a trailer, and having a dysfunctional family, she became the laughingstock of her school growing up. Between living in a trailer and having her father as a trash man, it simply was a setup for disaster. However, she overcame all of her obstacles after meeting her current husband Eric May. He showed her what life was truly about, how to love unconditionally, and most importantly became the step-up father to both of her boys Aaryn and Corey.

Even though there are days I wish I could change some things that happened in the past, there is a reason the rearview mirror is so small, and the windshield is so big. Where you are headed is more important than what you left behind.

-UNKNOWN-

The Super Powered Mind

When someone starts blaming you after they have continually disrespected you and your boundaries and after you have repeatedly asked them not to; this is a major red flag!

Because they now know they are hurting you through their actions, yet they continue to do it.

They continue to be disrespectful towards you.

They continue to hurt you and your emotions and then blame you for it if you dare bring it up again.

This is manipulation!

Manipulation is real!

Emotional manipulation is real!

But an expert manipulator is a master at the art of being subtle.

It starts as a white lie here and there.

A couple of hurtful backhanded comments or comments that put you down.

They start twisting what you've said to make you start to doubt yourself.

Then the snide comments start to escalate.

They start accusing you of changing your mind all the time to make you feel like your behavior is irrational and confusing when all you are trying to do is keep up with their ever-changing demands.

They lie to you and then deflect when you try to discuss it with them.

They become defensive when you present the evidence to them.

They start to use your values and your love languages against you to emotionally manipulate you.

They will tell you not to turn things around onto because everything is your fault.

And before you know it, it snowballs into a world of chaos where suddenly, they are convincing everyone else that you are the problem.

All because you dared to confront them about their disrespect.

But because you have confronted them, they now feel like they have lost their control over you, because you've figured out what they've been doing to you.

So, they now turn their attention to controlling how everyone else sees you.

They will stop at nothing and no one to ensure that their carefully crafted image isn't tarnished and that their ego isn't damaged.
They will create false stories about you, and they will twist the truth so much that it no longer resembles the truth.
They will even go as far as to label you as their manipulator, their narcissist.
They paint themselves as the innocent victim when they in fact have been the perpetrators all along.
And because they are so particularly good at what they do, they go undetected.
They are covert!
Because they know how to play the game because they have done it multiple times before.
But behind the mask lies the truth.
The truth that you KNOW to be real.
And the person that they are that no one else sees...
They are toxic. They are gaslighting you.
They are manipulating you!
There is no reason with someone like this because they can never be wrong.
If this sounds familiar to you, do yourself a favor and see it for what it is.
Because whilst they might not admit to it or agree, this IS manipulation...
And the longer you allow it to continue, the higher they increase their threshold for hurting you and destroying your self-esteem and self-worth.
And I don't know about you, but this doesn't sound like love to me...
Because when you love someone, this isn't how you treat them...
-MARK-

"Narcissists try to destroy your life with lies because theirs can be destroyed with the truth. They are like fragile glass sculptures - beautiful on the outside, but hollow and brittle on the inside. They are terrified that one wrong move, one harsh word, one revealing truth will shatter their delicate facade and expose their emptiness.

So, they attack, they smear, they slander. They weave a web of deceit and manipulation, hoping to ensnare you in their trap of lies. They will stop at nothing to discredit you, to humiliate you, to annihilate you.

But here's the thing: their lives are like sandcastles in the ocean - fragile, ephemeral, and easily washed away. And the truth? The truth is like a rock, solid, unshakeable, and unbreakable.

The truth will always prevail, no matter how hard the narcissist tries to bury it. The truth will always rise to the surface, no matter how much they try to suppress it. And when it does, their house of cards will come crashing down, their lies will be exposed, and their true nature will be revealed.

So do not be afraid, don't be intimidated, don't be silenced. Speak the truth, share the truth, live the truth. For the truth is your shield, your sword, your superpower. And with it, you'll be the one who'll ultimately destroy their lies, their manipulation, and their destructive power."

-UNKNOWN-

Narcissist's Daughter

The act of walking away from someone you love is not a surrender, but a profound reclamation of the self – a defiant declaration that your well-being, your peace, and your very survival, are sacrosanct and worthy of fierce protection.

For those who have had to make this agonizing choice, you know the depths of courage it demands. To turn your back on the familiar, on the bonds that once tethered you, to safeguard the fragile flame of your existence – it is a revolution of the soul, a refusal to let your light be extinguished by the forces that seek to diminish you.

In that pivotal moment, when the scales finally tipped and you realized that staying would be an act of self-annihilation, you made the brave choice to put your oxygen mask on first. You chose to honor the truth that self-preservation is not selfish, but a radical act of self-love and self-respect.

And in doing so, you unlocked a deeper understanding of what it truly means to cherish yourself – not just in words, but in actions that demand your priorities your well-being above all else. How can we claim to love ourselves if we willingly remain in situations that erode our peace, our boundaries, and our fundamental sense of worth?

This journey has been one of profound growth, of shedding the narratives that kept you tethered to cycles of self-abandonment and people-pleasing. It has been a reclamation of your sovereignty, a defiant stance against the notion that your needs should ever be subjugated for the sake of others.

So let this be a celebration of your resilience, of the self-love and self-respect that guided you through the fire and into the light. Let it be a reminder that walking away from what no longer serves you is not defeat, but the ultimate act of self-preservation – a choice that honors the sacred truth that you, and you alone, are the author of your becoming.

-UNKNOWN

You Took My Childhood Away

I was a tiny child.

So innocent and mild

You told me to play a game.

Did you have no shame?

You said not to tell my mother.

You said not to tell my dad.

You said it was a secret.

And if I told you I'd make you sad

How could you do that to a child?

Who was placed in your care?

And how can you live with what you've done?

The past to think about how can you bear?

What gave you the right? To use a child for your dirty game?

For hurting a child inside

Or will the things you've said and done?

Will you, always hide?

How can you mess up a mind?

Of a child who trusted you?

How can you live with what you've done?

It was wrong, surely you knew.

You've never said you're sorry.

I'm haunted every day.

Of what you did to me

And how you hurt me in that way.

You betrayed the trust.

Of a little girl in your care

At you, if I saw you again in the street I'd shout and swear

At times I feel so rotten

But I'm told it wasn't my fault.

But I feel like I'm involved.

Like pepper is to salt

I was four years old Just out of nappies, couldn't you see?

I sit alone at night.

And ask, "Oh why was it me?"

All I can do now is try to get on.

But I can't ever forget.

And my children under someone else's care

It is something I will NEVER let.

Poem by Payge Rogers

Thank You

Stay tuned for the sequel of *Children Should Be Seen and Not Heard, Breaking The Silence* it will be released in 2025. The book is called Children Should Be Seen and Not Heard Breaking the Family Cycle.

www.ingramcontent.com/pod-product-compliance
Lightning Source LLC
Chambersburg PA
CBHW051956220626
47052CB00004B/971